The Enchanted Mirror

Fairy tales, Folk tales, Legends & Mythology, Volume 6

Patrick William Lee

Published by Starlit Tales Publishing, 2024.

THE ENCHANTED MIRROR

First edition. September 2, 2024.

ISBN: 979-8227008367

Written by Patrick William Lee.

Table of Contents

To those who dare to dream beyond the ordinary and embrace the extraordinary path set before them. May you always find the courage to seek your own truth, the strength to face your deepest fears, and the wisdom to fulfill your destiny.

And to my companions in life's journey—family, friends, and all those who have stood by me through the trials and triumphs—this tale is as much yours as it is mine. Thank you for your unwavering support and belief in the magic of storytelling.

This book is for you.

Chapter 1: The Prophecy Foretold

The kingdom of Eldoria was a land shrouded in mystery and bathed in the golden hues of legend. Its towering peaks kissed the heavens, while the valleys below cradled forests of emerald green, thick with ancient trees that whispered secrets to those who dared to listen. Rivers of crystal-clear water wove through the landscape, their gentle currents singing songs of forgotten times. Eldoria was a kingdom where the mundane and the magical coexisted, where the air itself seemed to shimmer with the remnants of ancient spells. It was a land where stories were not merely told but lived, where legends walked among the people as surely as the sun rose each day.

In the heart of this mystical kingdom, nestled between the rolling hills and the edge of the Whispering Woods, lay the village of Briar Glen. It was a humble village, far removed from the grandeur of Eldoria's capital, Veridale. The villagers were simple folk, their lives intertwined with the rhythms of the earth—sowing, reaping, and tending to the land that had sustained them for generations. The houses of Briar Glen were modest, their thatched roofs and wooden walls standing as testament to the villagers' connection with nature. Smoke curled lazily from chimneys, mingling with the morning mist, as the first light of dawn broke over the horizon.

It was here, in this unassuming village, that the tale of destiny began—a tale that would change the fate of the entire kingdom.

Elara, the daughter of a simple farmer, lived in a small cottage on the outskirts of Briar Glen. Her life was one of routine and quiet contentment. Each day, she would rise before the sun, her hands quick and skillful as she prepared the morning meal for her aging father. Afterward, she would tend to the chickens in their coop, their soft clucking a familiar soundtrack to her morning chores. The rest of her day was spent in the fields, where she toiled alongside her father, planting seeds, pulling weeds, and harvesting the fruits of their labor.

Elara's mother had passed away when she was just a child, leaving her father, Gareth, to raise her alone. Gareth was a man of few words, but his love for his daughter was evident in every glance, every gesture. Though their lives were simple, they were rich in the love and companionship they shared. Elara had never known the luxury of the city or the excitement of adventure, but she had never felt the lack of it. Her world was small, but it was enough—until the day the oracle came to Briar Glen.

It was the time of the Harvest Festival, a celebration that marked the end of the growing season and the beginning of the harvest. The village square was alive with color and sound, the air thick with the scent of roasting meats and the sweet fragrance of freshly baked bread. Children ran through the streets, their laughter echoing off the stone walls of the village hall, where the elders sat in council. Musicians played lively tunes on their fiddles and flutes, and the villagers danced with abandon, their faces flushed with joy.

Elara stood on the edge of the square, her eyes bright as she watched the festivities. She had always loved the Harvest Festival, the one time of year when the whole village came together in celebration. Her father was somewhere in the crowd, likely sharing a drink and a story with old friends. Elara herself had danced for a while, but now she found herself content to simply watch, her heart light and her spirit free.

It was then that the oracle arrived.

The music faltered, the dancers stilled, and the laughter died on the villagers' lips as a hush fell over the square. All eyes turned toward the edge of the village, where a figure stood, draped in a cloak of midnight blue, the hood pulled low over their face. The oracle was a being of legend, a mysterious figure who appeared only when the kingdom was on the brink of great change. Some said the oracle was as old as time itself, a being who had walked the earth since the dawn of creation. Others whispered that the oracle was not one being, but many, each passing the mantle of prophecy from one to the next. Whatever the truth, the presence of the oracle in Briar Glen was a sign that something momentous was about to unfold.

The villagers parted like the sea before the oracle, their heads bowed in reverence and fear. The oracle moved with a grace that seemed almost otherworldly, their steps silent as they approached the center of the square. When they reached the village well, the oracle stopped and lowered their hood, revealing a face that was both ageless and timeless. Their eyes, a shade of deep violet, held the weight of countless lifetimes, and when they spoke, their voice was like the rustling of leaves in a forgotten forest.

"People of Briar Glen," the oracle intoned, their voice carrying across the square. "A time of great change is upon us. The winds of destiny are shifting, and the fate of our kingdom hangs in the balance."

A murmur rippled through the crowd, a mixture of awe and apprehension. The villagers knew that when the oracle spoke, their words were not to be taken lightly. Prophecies were rare, and when they came, they were often the harbingers of both great joy and great sorrow.

Elara felt a shiver run down her spine as she listened to the oracle's words. There was something in the air, something that made her heart race and her palms sweat. She glanced around the square, searching for her father, but the crowd was too thick. She turned her attention back to the oracle, unable to tear her eyes away.

"The Mirror of Eldoria," the oracle continued, "an artifact of immense power, has been lost for generations. It is said that the mirror holds the power to reveal one's true destiny, to show the path that lies ahead. But the mirror is more than just a tool of prophecy—it is a key, a gateway to a future that is yet unwritten. And now, the time has come for the mirror to be found, for the destiny of Eldoria to be revealed."

A collective gasp rose from the villagers, their eyes wide with shock and wonder. The Mirror of Eldoria was a legend, a story told to children at bedtime. It was said to have been created by the first king of Eldoria, a wise and just ruler who had used the mirror to guide his kingdom through times of peace and war. But the mirror had been lost after the king's death, and no one had seen it since. Many believed it was just a myth, a fairy tale to entertain the young and the foolish.

But the oracle's presence made it clear that the mirror was real, and its rediscovery was imminent.

"There is one among you," the oracle said, their eyes scanning the crowd, "who holds the key to finding the mirror. This person's destiny is intertwined with the fate of the kingdom. They must embark on a journey, a quest to uncover the mirror and bring it back to its rightful place."

Elara's heart skipped a beat. A quest? A journey to find the Mirror of Eldoria? It sounded like something out of the stories her mother used to tell her as a child. She had always dreamed of adventure, of stepping beyond the boundaries of Briar Glen and seeing the world beyond. But she had never imagined that such a destiny could be hers.

The oracle's gaze swept across the villagers, their eyes lingering on each face as if searching for something unseen. Elara held her breath, hoping and fearing in equal measure that the oracle's gaze would land on her. But the oracle's eyes passed over her, moving on to the next villager and the next.

"The one who is destined to find the mirror," the oracle said, "will know it in their heart. They will feel the call of destiny, the pull of the unknown. And when they do, they must answer it, for the fate of Eldoria depends on it."

The oracle's words hung in the air like a heavy mist, wrapping around the villagers and seeping into their souls. For a moment, no one moved or spoke, each person lost in their own thoughts, wondering if they were the one the oracle had spoken of.

Elara felt a strange sensation in her chest, a warmth that spread through her body and settled in her heart. It was as if something had awakened within her, something that had been dormant for years. She placed a hand over her heart, feeling its steady beat, and wondered if this was the call of destiny the oracle had spoken of.

But before she could dwell on it further, the oracle raised their hand, and the crowd fell silent once more.

"The journey will not be easy," the oracle warned. "The mirror is hidden in a far-off land, guarded by forces both powerful and ancient. The one who seeks it must be strong of heart and pure of spirit. They will face trials and challenges that will test their very soul. But if they succeed, they will not only find the mirror—they will find their true self."

With those final words, the oracle turned and began to walk away, their cloak billowing behind them like a shadow. The villagers watched in stunned silence as the oracle disappeared into the mist that had begun to gather at the edge of the village. It was only when the oracle was out of sight that the spell seemed to break, and the villagers began to murmur among themselves, their voices a mix of excitement and fear.

Elara stood rooted to the spot, her mind racing with the possibilities that the oracle's words had opened up. Could it be true? Could she be the one destined to find the Mirror of Eldoria? It seemed impossible, yet the warmth in her chest persisted, a constant reminder that something within her had changed.

She needed to find her father. She needed to talk to him, to tell him what she had felt, and to hear his thoughts on the matter. But as she turned to leave the square, a hand caught her arm, stopping her in her tracks.

"Elara."

She looked up to see the village elder, a kindly old woman named Anwen, standing before her. Anwen's eyes were sharp, despite her age, and they seemed to pierce through Elara's very soul.

"Elara," Anwen said again, her voice gentle but firm. "I need to speak with you."

Elara nodded, her heart still racing. "Of course, Elder Anwen. What is it?"

Anwen glanced around, ensuring that no one was close enough to overhear. "Not here," she said. "Come with me."

Without another word, Anwen led Elara away from the square and toward the edge of the village, where a small cottage stood, half-hidden by the trees. It was Anwen's home, a place Elara had visited many times as a child. Anwen had always been kind to her, offering her sweets and stories whenever she came to visit. But there was a seriousness in Anwen's demeanor now that Elara had never seen before, and it made her nervous.

When they reached the cottage, Anwen opened the door and gestured for Elara to enter. The inside of the cottage was warm and inviting, the walls lined with shelves filled with jars of herbs and bottles of potions. A fire crackled in the hearth, casting flickering shadows on the walls. Anwen motioned for Elara to sit at the small wooden table in the center of the room, and Elara did so, her hands clasped tightly in her lap.

Anwen sat across from her, her eyes never leaving Elara's face. For a long moment, she said nothing, simply studying the young woman before her. Finally, she spoke.

"Elara," she began, her voice soft but filled with an urgency that made Elara's heart skip a beat. "Do you know why I brought you here?"

Elara shook her head, though a part of her already suspected the answer. "No, Elder Anwen."

Anwen nodded, as if she had expected as much. "The oracle's prophecy... it is not the first time I have heard of it. The Mirror of Eldoria is real, and its power is beyond anything you can imagine. But it is also dangerous, Elara. Many have sought it, but none have succeeded in finding it. And those who have tried... they have paid a terrible price."

Elara swallowed, her throat suddenly dry. "But... but the oracle said that someone in the village would find it. That someone's destiny is tied to the mirror. Could it be me, Elder Anwen? Could I be the one?"

Anwen sighed, her eyes filled with both sadness and resolve. "Elara, I have watched you grow from a child into a young woman. You have always been special, though you may not know it. There is a strength in you, a light that shines even in the darkest of times. I have seen it, and I have always known that you were destined for something greater than this village."

Elara's heart pounded in her chest. "You think I'm the one, don't you?"

Anwen reached across the table and took Elara's hands in hers, her grip surprisingly strong for someone so old. "I do," she said quietly. "But that does not mean you should go. The journey to find the mirror will be fraught with danger. You will face trials that will test your very soul. And there is no guarantee that you will return."

Elara looked down at their joined hands, her mind a whirlwind of emotions. She had always dreamed of adventure, of stepping beyond the boundaries of Briar Glen and seeing the world beyond. But now that the opportunity was before her, she felt a pang of fear. Could she really do it? Could she leave behind everything she had ever known to seek out a legend?

"What should I do?" Elara asked, her voice barely above a whisper.

Anwen squeezed her hands gently. "That is not for me to decide, Elara. Only you can choose your path. But know this: if you choose to go, you will not be alone. There are those who will help you, guide you on your journey. And I will be here, waiting for your return."

Elara took a deep breath, trying to steady her racing heart. She could feel the warmth in her chest growing stronger, as if her very soul was urging her to accept the call of destiny. But the fear was still there, lurking in the back of her mind, whispering doubts and uncertainties.

"I... I need to think about it," Elara said finally, pulling her hands back and rising from the table. "I need to talk to my father."

Anwen nodded, her expression understanding. "Of course. Take all the time you need, Elara. But remember, the winds of destiny are already shifting. Whatever choice you make, do so with a clear heart."

Elara nodded, though her heart felt anything but clear. She thanked Anwen and left the cottage, her mind a jumble of thoughts as she made her way back to the village square. The festivities had resumed, though the mood was more subdued than before. The villagers were still abuzz with talk of the oracle's prophecy, their faces alight with both excitement and fear.

Elara searched the crowd for her father, finally spotting him near the edge of the square, talking with a group of old friends. She made her way over to him, her steps quickening as she drew closer.

"Father," she called out, her voice trembling slightly.

Gareth turned to see her, his weathered face breaking into a smile. "Elara, there you are. I was wondering where you'd gone off to."

Elara forced a smile, though her heart was heavy with the weight of the decision she knew she had to make. "Father, I... I need to talk to you. It's important."

Gareth's smile faded, his eyes narrowing with concern. "What is it, lass? You look troubled."

Elara glanced around, seeing that the other villagers were watching them with curious eyes. "Not here," she said, lowering her voice. "Can we go home?"

Gareth nodded, sensing the urgency in her tone. He bid his friends farewell and led Elara away from the square, his hand resting on her shoulder in a comforting gesture.

The walk back to their cottage was silent, the only sound the crunch of gravel beneath their feet. Elara's mind was racing, her thoughts a chaotic tangle of fear, hope, and uncertainty. She had always trusted her father's wisdom, and she hoped that he would be able to help her make sense of the whirlwind of emotions that was threatening to overwhelm her.

When they reached the cottage, Gareth opened the door and gestured for Elara to enter. She stepped inside, the familiar warmth of the hearth and the scent of herbs calming her frayed nerves. Gareth followed, closing the door behind him and turning to face his daughter.

"Now, Elara," he said, his voice gentle but firm. "Tell me what's troubling you."

Elara took a deep breath, trying to steady her racing heart. She could feel the warmth in her chest growing stronger, as if her very soul was urging her to accept the call of destiny. But the fear was still there, lurking in the back of her mind, whispering doubts and uncertainties.

She looked up at her father, her eyes searching his weathered face for any sign of what he might think of her decision. Gareth's eyes were kind, filled with the same quiet strength that had always been her anchor in times of trouble.

"Father," she began, her voice trembling slightly, "you heard the oracle's prophecy today. They spoke of the Mirror of Eldoria, and how someone in the village is destined to find it. I... I think that someone might be me."

Gareth's eyes widened slightly, but he said nothing, waiting for Elara to continue.

"I don't know how to explain it," Elara went on, her words tumbling out in a rush. "But when the oracle spoke, I felt something inside me. It was like a warmth, a pull, as if my heart was telling me that I'm the one they were talking about. Elder Anwen thinks so too. She said that she's always known I was destined for something greater."

Gareth remained silent, his expression unreadable.

"But I'm scared, Father," Elara admitted, her voice breaking. "The journey to find the mirror will be dangerous. The oracle said I would face trials that would test my very soul. What if I'm not strong enough? What if I fail?"

Gareth sighed deeply, his eyes softening with understanding. He crossed the room and took his daughter's hands in his, his grip warm and reassuring.

"Elara," he said gently, "I won't pretend to understand the ways of destiny or the power of prophecy. But I do know one thing: you are stronger than you think. You have a light in you, a strength that has carried you through every hardship life has thrown your way. And if this is your destiny, then I believe with all my heart that you will find the courage to face whatever lies ahead."

Tears welled up in Elara's eyes, but she blinked them back, nodding slowly. "I want to believe that, Father. I want to believe that I'm meant for something more. But it's so hard. I've never left this village. I've never been on an adventure, never faced anything more dangerous than a storm or a sick chicken. How can I possibly be the one to find the mirror?"

Gareth smiled softly, his eyes filled with pride. "You may have lived a simple life, Elara, but that doesn't mean you're not capable of great things. You've always had a sense of wonder, a curiosity about the world beyond Briar Glen. And now, it seems, the world is calling you. I can't tell you what to do, but I can tell you this: whatever choice you make, I will support you. Whether you stay or go, you will always have a home here, and you will always have my love."

Elara's heart swelled with emotion, the fear and uncertainty that had been gnawing at her beginning to fade in the face of her father's unwavering support. She squeezed his hands, drawing strength from his words.

"Thank you, Father," she whispered. "I don't know what I'll do yet, but it helps to know that you believe in me."

Gareth nodded, releasing her hands and stepping back. "Take your time, Elara. There's no rush to decide. The oracle's prophecy may have set things in motion, but the choice is yours. And whatever you choose, remember that you are stronger than you know."

Elara nodded, her mind still racing but her heart a little lighter. She knew that she had a decision to make, one that could change her life—and the fate of the kingdom—forever. But she also knew that, whatever she chose, she would not be alone. She had her father's love, Elder Anwen's guidance, and a light within her that had yet to be fully realized.

The night passed slowly, the weight of the decision pressing heavily on Elara's mind. She tossed and turned in her bed, her thoughts a whirlwind of possibilities. But as the first light of dawn began to filter through her window, she made her decision.

She would answer the call of destiny.

With a newfound resolve, Elara rose from her bed and dressed quickly. She would need to prepare for the journey ahead, gather supplies, and say her goodbyes. But first, there was something she needed to do.

She left the cottage and made her way to the village square, where the last remnants of the Harvest Festival were being cleared away. The sun was just beginning to rise, casting a golden glow over the village. The air was cool and crisp, filled with the scent of autumn leaves.

Elara approached the well in the center of the square, the place where the oracle had stood the day before. She took a deep breath and knelt before the well, closing her eyes and bowing her head.

"Oracle," she whispered, her voice trembling slightly. "I don't know if you can hear me, but I've made my decision. I will seek the Mirror of Eldoria. I will accept the challenge, face the trials, and find my true destiny. I don't know what lies ahead, but I am ready to follow the path you have set before me."

As she spoke, the warmth in her chest flared, spreading through her body like a beacon of light. It was as if the very air around her was responding to her words, filling her with a sense of purpose and determination.

When she opened her eyes, she found that she was no longer alone.

Standing before her was a figure draped in a cloak of midnight blue, their hood pulled low over their face. The oracle had returned.

Elara gasped, her heart pounding in her chest. She had not expected to see the oracle again, not so soon. But the figure before her was unmistakable—the same presence, the same aura of power and mystery.

"Elara," the oracle said, their voice like the rustling of leaves in a forgotten forest. "You have made your choice."

Elara nodded, her throat too tight to speak.

The oracle reached out a hand, and Elara felt a gentle warmth as their fingers brushed her cheek. "You have a long journey ahead of you, Elara. But you are not alone. The path will be difficult, but you have the strength to see it through. Trust in yourself, and trust in those who will walk beside you."

Elara nodded again, feeling a surge of courage and resolve. "I will do my best, Oracle. I will not fail."

The oracle smiled, their eyes filled with a deep, ancient wisdom. "I know you won't. You are destined for greatness, Elara. And when the time comes, you will understand the true power of the mirror—and the true power within yourself."

With those words, the oracle stepped back, their form beginning to fade into the morning mist. "Go now, Elara. Your destiny awaits."

And with that, the oracle was gone, leaving Elara alone in the square.

But she no longer felt alone. The warmth in her chest was a constant presence, a reminder of the path she had chosen. She would find the Mirror of

Eldoria. She would face the trials, overcome the challenges, and discover her true destiny.

And as she stood in the square, the first rays of sunlight breaking over the horizon, Elara knew that her journey was only just beginning.

End of Chapter 1.

Chapter 2: The Call to Adventure

The days that followed the oracle's visit were unsettling for Elara. The once comforting routines of her life now seemed shadowed by the weight of the prophecy. The fields where she had always felt at peace, where the scent of earth and the rhythm of her father's voice had brought her solace, now felt different—tinged with an unease she could not shake. The oracle's words echoed in her mind, haunting her thoughts even as she tried to focus on the work at hand.

Elara's father, Gareth, noticed the change in his daughter. He saw how she moved through her tasks with a distracted air, her eyes often drifting toward the distant horizon as if searching for something just out of reach. She no longer hummed the familiar tunes that had once filled the air as she worked, and her laughter, which had once been so frequent and full of life, had grown rare. Gareth's heart ached for her, knowing that she was wrestling with something far greater than any challenge she had faced before.

The villagers of Briar Glen, too, sensed that something was different about Elara. They whispered among themselves, their gazes lingering on her longer than before. Some spoke of the prophecy with awe, convinced that their quiet village was now at the center of a great and wondrous tale. Others were more wary, fearful of what such a prophecy might mean for them all. But none dared to approach Elara directly, for she had become an enigma, a figure both familiar and foreign, touched by forces they could not understand.

Elara tried to push the thoughts of the prophecy from her mind, to immerse herself in the tasks that had always given her purpose. But no matter how hard she tried, she could not escape the strange dreams that began to plague her each night.

In these dreams, she found herself standing on the edge of a vast and ancient forest, its trees so tall that their tops seemed to pierce the sky. The air was thick with the scent of moss and earth, and the only sound was the rustling of leaves in a wind that seemed to come from nowhere. In her dream, Elara would take a step forward, into the forest, and as she did, the trees would seem to close in around her, their branches reaching out like skeletal fingers. Shadows flitted at the edges of her vision, and though she could not see them clearly, she knew they were watching her, waiting for her to venture deeper into their domain.

Each night, the dream would progress a little further. She would walk deeper into the forest, the shadows growing thicker and the sense of unease more oppressive. Yet she felt a strange compulsion to keep going, to follow a path that seemed to wind through the trees like a serpent, leading her toward something she could not yet see. And always, just as she felt she was about to reach the heart of the forest, she would awaken with a start, her heart pounding in her chest, her body drenched in sweat.

The dreams left her shaken, and she could not help but wonder if they were more than just figments of her imagination. The oracle had spoken of destiny, of a journey she was meant to undertake. Could these dreams be a sign, a message from the forces that guided her fate? The thought both frightened and intrigued her, and she found herself longing for answers that seemed just out of reach.

It was on a particularly cool autumn morning, as the first hints of winter began to creep into the air, that the old sage arrived in Briar Glen.

The villagers had seen the sage before, though rarely, for his visits were infrequent and often shrouded in mystery. He was known simply as Valen, a man of indeterminate age, with hair as white as the snow that blanketed the kingdom in winter. His eyes were a piercing blue, sharp and clear, with a depth that spoke of wisdom gained over many lifetimes. Valen traveled the land, offering his counsel to those who sought it and sharing the knowledge he had gleaned from his many years of study. But there was an air of the otherworldly about him, a sense that he was more than just a man—that he was somehow connected to the ancient forces that shaped the world.

When Valen arrived in Briar Glen, the villagers watched with a mixture of curiosity and trepidation. He walked with a staff of polished oak, its surface carved with intricate runes that seemed to glow faintly in the dim light. His cloak, a deep shade of green, billowed behind him as he moved, blending with the autumn foliage that blanketed the village. Though he moved slowly, with the deliberate grace of one who knew the weight of each step, there was a power in his presence that commanded attention.

Elara was in the fields when she first saw the sage. She had been working to gather the last of the harvest, her thoughts once again drifting to the strange dreams that had plagued her the night before, when she looked up and saw him standing at the edge of the field, watching her with those sharp, blue eyes. For a moment, she thought she was still dreaming, for the sight of him seemed so surreal, so unexpected. But as she blinked and the image remained, she realized that this was no dream—Valen was here, in Briar Glen, and he was looking directly at her.

The sage said nothing at first, simply studying her with an intensity that made her heart race. Elara felt a shiver run down her spine, though whether it was from fear or something else, she could not say. She stood frozen in place, unsure of what to do, until Valen finally spoke.

"Elara," he said, his voice low and resonant, carrying across the field with ease. "I have been waiting for you."

Elara's breath caught in her throat. The sage's words, though simple, carried with them the weight of destiny, and she knew at once that this was no ordinary encounter. Gathering her courage, she set down the basket she had been carrying and made her way toward him, her steps hesitant at first, but growing surer with each stride.

As she drew closer, she could see the lines etched into Valen's face, the marks of a life lived long and well. There was kindness in his eyes, but also a deep seriousness, a gravity that reminded her of the oracle's visit not long before. When she reached him, she paused, unsure of how to address him, but Valen gave her a small, reassuring smile.

"You need not be afraid, child," he said, his voice gentler now. "I have come to help you, to guide you on the path that lies ahead."

Elara swallowed, her heart still pounding in her chest. "The path to the Mirror of Eldoria?" she asked, her voice barely above a whisper.

Valen nodded, his expression grave. "Yes. The oracle has spoken, and the signs are clear. You are the one destined to find the mirror, Elara. But the journey will be long and perilous, and you must be prepared for what lies ahead."

Elara felt a lump form in her throat, the fear she had been trying to suppress rising once more. "But... how can I do this? I'm just a farmer's daughter. I've never traveled beyond Briar Glen. How can I possibly find something that has been lost for generations?"

Valen's gaze softened, and he reached out to place a hand on her shoulder. "You are more than you know, Elara. There is a strength within you, a light that will guide you through the darkest of times. The mirror is not just a tool—it is a reflection of the soul, a revelation of one's true self. To find it, you must first find yourself."

Elara looked down at her hands, hands that were calloused and rough from years of labor. She had never thought of herself as anything more than a simple villager, a daughter who loved her father and her home. The idea that she might be destined for something greater, something far beyond the life she had always known, was both exhilarating and terrifying.

"What if I fail?" she asked, her voice trembling with the weight of her doubts.

Valen shook his head. "Failure is not the end, Elara. It is a part of the journey, a lesson to be learned. But you will not be alone in this. There are those who will stand by your side, who will help you face the challenges that lie ahead. And I will be here to offer my counsel whenever you need it."

Elara felt a tear slip down her cheek, though she quickly wiped it away. She knew that Valen's words were meant to reassure her, to give her the strength to accept her fate. But the fear still lingered, gnawing at the edges of her resolve.

"I don't know if I'm ready," she admitted, her voice barely audible.

Valen's hand tightened on her shoulder, his grip firm but comforting. "None of us are ever truly ready for the challenges life presents, Elara. But readiness is not the same as willingness. You have a choice to make, and that choice will shape the path that lies ahead. Do not think of yourself as unworthy or unprepared. Think of yourself as someone with the courage to take the first step."

Elara nodded, though the weight of the decision still hung heavily on her. She had known, ever since the oracle's visit, that this moment would come—that she would have to decide whether to embrace her destiny or to turn away from it. But now that the moment was here, the reality of it was almost too much to bear.

"I will try," she said finally, her voice stronger now. "I will do my best."

Valen smiled, a look of approval in his eyes. "That is all anyone can ask of you, Elara. And know this: your best will be enough. You are stronger than you know."

He released her shoulder and stepped back, his gaze never leaving hers. "There is much you need to do before you can begin your journey. You must gather supplies, say your goodbyes, and prepare yourself for what lies ahead. But first, there is something I must give you."

From within the folds of his cloak, Valen produced a small, ornate box, its surface covered in intricate carvings that glinted in the sunlight. He held it out to Elara, who took it with trembling hands.

"What is this?" she asked, her curiosity piqued.

Valen's expression grew serious. "It is a gift, one that has been passed down through generations, waiting for the one who is destined to find the mirror. Inside, you will find something that will guide you on your journey, something that will help you when the path seems darkest."

Elara's fingers traced the carvings on the box, feeling the cool, smooth surface beneath her touch. She could sense the power within it, a power that both frightened and fascinated her.

"Thank you," she said, her voice filled with gratitude.

Valen nodded, a hint of a smile returning to his lips. "Use it wisely, Elara. And remember, you are never truly alone. The forces of the world move in ways we cannot always see, but they are always there, guiding us, helping us to find our way."

With those words, Valen turned and began to walk away, his staff tapping lightly against the ground as he moved. Elara watched him go, feeling a strange mix of emotions—fear, hope, excitement, and a deep sense of responsibility.

As Valen disappeared into the distance, Elara looked down at the box in her hands. She knew that within it lay the first step of her journey, the first piece of the puzzle that would lead her to the Mirror of Eldoria. But she also knew that the journey ahead would not be easy—that it would test her in ways she could not yet imagine.

With a deep breath, she turned and began to walk back to the cottage, her mind racing with thoughts of what was to come. She would speak to her father, tell him of the decision she had made, and prepare for the journey that lay ahead. But she would do so with the knowledge that she was not alone—that there were forces at work, guiding her, helping her to find her true destiny.

ELARA SPENT THE REST of the day in a state of quiet determination, her mind focused on the tasks that needed to be done. She and her father worked together in the fields, gathering the last of the harvest and storing it away for the winter. The work was hard, but it provided a welcome distraction from the thoughts that had been swirling in her mind since Valen's visit.

As the sun began to set, casting a warm golden light over the village, Elara and her father returned to the cottage, their arms full of produce and their hearts full of unspoken words. Gareth could sense that something had shifted within his daughter—that she had made a decision, and that it was one that would change the course of her life. But he did not press her for details, knowing that she would speak when she was ready.

After they had finished their evening meal, Elara finally broached the subject that had been weighing on her heart.

"Father," she began, her voice soft but steady. "I've decided to go. I'm going to seek the Mirror of Eldoria."

Gareth looked at her for a long moment, his expression unreadable. Finally, he nodded, his eyes filled with a mixture of pride and sadness.

"I knew you would," he said quietly. "I knew, from the moment the oracle spoke, that you would accept your destiny. It's who you are, Elara. You've always had a spirit that reaches beyond the boundaries of this village, a curiosity that could never be confined to one place. I've always known that you were meant for something greater."

Elara felt a lump form in her throat, but she swallowed it down, determined to stay strong. "I'm scared, Father. I don't know what's going to happen, or if I'll be able to do this. But I know that I have to try."

Gareth reached across the table and took her hand in his, his grip warm and reassuring. "You're stronger than you think, Elara. And you have a light within you that will guide you through whatever lies ahead. I believe in you, and I know that you'll find the strength to face whatever challenges come your way."

Elara squeezed his hand, drawing comfort from his words. "Thank you, Father. Your support means everything to me."

Gareth smiled, though there was a hint of sadness in his eyes. "I'll miss you, Elara. But I know that this is something you have to do. And I'll be here, waiting for you when you return."

Elara nodded, her heart heavy with the knowledge that she would soon be leaving the only home she had ever known. But she also knew that this was her path—that she had been chosen for a reason, and that she had to see it through.

Over the next few days, Elara and her father worked together to prepare for her journey. They gathered supplies—food, water, a sturdy cloak to protect her from the elements, and a small knife for protection. Elara packed her belongings carefully, her hands moving with a sense of purpose that belied the turmoil in her heart.

The villagers, too, came to offer their support. Though they were sad to see her go, they understood the importance of her journey, and they provided her with whatever they could spare—dried meats, herbs for healing, and a small flask of strong spirits to ward off the chill of the night. They spoke to her in hushed tones, their words filled with both fear and hope, and they wished her well, knowing that she carried the fate of the kingdom on her shoulders.

On the morning of her departure, Elara stood at the edge of the village, her father by her side. The sun had just begun to rise, casting a golden light over the landscape, and the air was cool and crisp, filled with the scent of autumn leaves.

Elara took a deep breath, her heart heavy with the weight of the journey that lay ahead. She looked at her father, her eyes filled with a mixture of sadness and determination.

"I'll be back, Father," she said, her voice strong and clear. "I promise."

Gareth nodded, his eyes misty with unshed tears. "I know you will, Elara. And I'll be here, waiting for you."

With one last embrace, Elara turned and began to walk away from the village, her steps steady and sure. She could feel the weight of the box Valen had given her in her pack, a reminder of the destiny that awaited her. The path ahead was uncertain, filled with unknown dangers and challenges, but she knew that she had to face it with courage and resolve.

As she walked, the village grew smaller and smaller behind her, until it was just a distant memory, a place she had once called home. But she did not look back. She kept her eyes fixed on the horizon, on the path that lay ahead, knowing that this was the beginning of a journey that would change her life forever.

And as she walked, she felt a strange sense of peace settle over her—a sense that, no matter what happened, she was exactly where she was meant to be.

End of Chapter 2.

Chapter 3: The Gathering of Allies

Elara's journey had begun, and with each step away from Briar Glen, the familiarity of her village life faded into the background. The road ahead was unknown, and the weight of the prophecy sat heavily on her shoulders. The world beyond her home was vast and filled with mysteries she could only begin to imagine. Yet, as daunting as the task before her seemed, she knew one thing for certain—she could not do this alone.

The first few days of her journey were uneventful, though not without their challenges. Elara was unaccustomed to the solitude of the open road. The silence, broken only by the sounds of nature—the rustling of leaves, the distant cry of a hawk, the soft whisper of the wind—was both comforting and unnerving. She had only the thoughts in her head to keep her company, and they often spiraled into doubts and fears about the path she had chosen.

The road wound through dense forests and across wide, open fields, the landscape shifting from the familiar greens and browns of her home to the more varied hues of the kingdom beyond. The days were long, and the nights were cold, but Elara pressed on, driven by the knowledge that she had a purpose, a destiny that she could not turn away from.

On the fifth day, as the sun began to dip below the horizon, casting the world in a golden light, Elara found herself approaching a small town nestled in a valley. The town, known as Grayridge, was surrounded by rolling hills and lush farmland, its stone buildings huddled together as if for warmth. Smoke rose from chimneys, and the scent of baked bread and roasting meat wafted through the air, making Elara's stomach growl in response.

As she entered the town, the villagers eyed her with a mix of curiosity and caution. Travelers were not uncommon in Grayridge, but Elara's determined stride and the cloak that billowed behind her suggested she was not just another passing wanderer. She made her way to the town's inn, a modest building with a thatched roof and a sign that swung gently in the breeze, creaking on its hinges. The sign bore the image of a horse rearing on its hind legs, and the words "The Silver Stallion" were painted in faded gold.

Elara pushed open the heavy wooden door and stepped inside, the warmth of the inn enveloping her like a blanket. The common room was bustling with activity—patrons sat at wooden tables, talking and laughing over mugs of ale, while a fire crackled in the hearth, casting flickering shadows on the walls. The scent of roasting meat mingled with the aroma of spiced cider, and Elara's mouth watered at the thought of a hot meal.

She approached the innkeeper, a burly man with a thick beard and a friendly smile, who was wiping down the bar with a rag.

"Good evening," she said, her voice steady despite the nerves that fluttered in her stomach. "I'm looking for a room for the night."

The innkeeper looked her up and down, his eyes lingering on the worn edges of her cloak and the travel dust that clung to her boots. "Aye, we've got rooms," he said with a nod. "But we're nearly full. You're in luck—just one room left."

Elara smiled gratefully. "That will do. Thank you."

The innkeeper reached behind the bar and pulled out a key, handing it to her with a nod toward the stairs at the back of the room. "Up the stairs, second door on the left. Supper's still hot if you're hungry."

Elara took the key and slipped it into her pocket. "Thank you," she repeated, turning toward the stairs. But before she could take more than a few steps, a voice called out from one of the tables near the hearth.

"Traveler! Join us, won't you?"

Elara paused, turning to see who had spoken. The voice belonged to a man sitting with a group of others at a table near the fire. He was tall and broad-shouldered, with a mane of dark hair that framed a ruggedly handsome face. His eyes sparkled with mischief, and a roguish grin tugged at the corners of his mouth. He raised a mug of ale in her direction, his invitation clear.

The others at the table—two men and a woman—turned to look at her, their expressions curious but not unfriendly. Elara hesitated for a moment, but the thought of sitting alone in her room, eating a solitary meal, did not appeal to her. With a small nod, she made her way over to the table.

As she approached, the man who had called out to her stood and pulled out a chair, gesturing for her to sit. "There's no need to dine alone, especially on a night like this," he said, his voice warm and inviting. "We're all travelers here, after all."

Elara smiled and took the offered seat, setting her pack down beside her. "Thank you," she said, grateful for the company. "I'm Elara."

"Ah, a pleasure to meet you, Elara," the man said with a grin. "I'm Dain." He gestured to the others at the table. "And these fine folks are Breck, Lyra, and Tomas."

Breck was a burly man with a thick beard and a no-nonsense demeanor. He nodded gruffly at Elara, his eyes appraising her with a mix of curiosity and caution. Lyra, the woman, was slender and graceful, with sharp features and eyes that seemed to take in everything around her. She gave Elara a small smile, her expression guarded but not unfriendly. Tomas, the youngest of the group, was lean and wiry, with a mop of unruly hair and an easygoing smile that put Elara at ease.

Elara nodded in greeting to each of them. "It's nice to meet you all."

Dain waved over a serving girl, who brought Elara a mug of ale and a plate of stew. "So, what brings you to Grayridge, Elara?" he asked, his tone casual but his eyes sharp with interest.

Elara hesitated for a moment, unsure of how much to reveal. The prophecy and her quest were not things she wanted to discuss with strangers—at least not until she knew more about them. But something about Dain's open and friendly demeanor made her feel that she could trust him, at least enough to give a vague answer.

"I'm traveling," she said simply, taking a sip of the ale. It was strong and bitter, but it warmed her insides pleasantly. "I have some... personal business to attend to."

Dain raised an eyebrow, his grin widening. "Personal business, eh? That sounds mysterious."

Elara smiled, grateful that he didn't press for more details. "What about you? Are you all traveling together?"

"Aye, we are," Dain said, leaning back in his chair. "Though we're a rather motley crew, as you can see." He glanced around the table, his expression fond. "We've been on the road for a while now, each of us with our own reasons for traveling. But we've found that it's better to travel with companions than to go it alone."

Elara nodded in agreement, her thoughts drifting to the road ahead. She knew that she would need help on her journey, and this group seemed capable and trustworthy—at least, as trustworthy as strangers could be.

"What about you, Elara?" Lyra asked, her voice soft but penetrating. "Where are you headed?"

Elara hesitated again, but then decided to be at least partially honest. "I'm on a journey to find something," she said, choosing her words carefully. "Something important."

Lyra's sharp eyes narrowed slightly, but she nodded. "I see. And do you plan to travel alone?"

Elara shook her head. "No, I don't think I can do it alone. But I haven't found the right companions yet."

Dain leaned forward, his grin turning into a thoughtful smile. "Well, it just so happens that we're looking for someone to join our merry band. We're heading toward the mountains, to the east. It's a dangerous road, full of bandits and other unsavory sorts. We could use someone with your... determination."

Elara looked at him, her heart skipping a beat. Was this fate, or merely coincidence? She had been seeking allies, and here they were, offering her a place among them. But could she trust them? Could she rely on them to help her in her quest?

She glanced around the table, meeting each of their gazes in turn. Breck's eyes were steady and serious, Lyra's sharp and calculating, and Tomas's bright with youthful enthusiasm. Dain, for all his roguish charm, had a look of genuine sincerity in his eyes. They were all strangers, yet she felt a strange sense of connection to them, as if they had been brought together for a reason.

Finally, she made her decision. "I would be honored to join you," she said, her voice firm. "But I must warn you—my journey will not be an easy one. There will be danger, and possibly more than you're prepared for."

Dain chuckled, his grin widening. "Elara, we live for danger. It's what keeps life interesting."

Breck grunted in agreement, and even Lyra allowed herself a small smile. Tomas raised his mug in a toast. "To new companions and new adventures!"

Elara smiled and lifted her mug, clinking it against the others'. "To new companions," she echoed, feeling a surge of hope and excitement.

As they drank, Dain leaned in closer, his expression more serious now. "Tell us, Elara—what is it that you're searching for? We may be able to help."

Elara hesitated for a moment, then decided that if they were to be her companions, they needed to know the truth. "I'm searching for the Mirror of Eldoria," she said, her voice low but steady. "It's an ancient artifact, said to reveal one's true destiny. It's been lost for generations, but I've been tasked with finding it."

Dain whistled softly, his eyes widening in surprise. "The Mirror of Eldoria? That's quite the quest you've undertaken."

Lyra's expression grew more guarded, but she nodded. "I've heard of it. They say it's hidden in a place where few dare to go, protected by powerful forces."

Breck grunted, his brow furrowing. "Sounds dangerous. But then, nothing worth having ever came easy."

Tomas's eyes were wide with excitement. "That sounds incredible! A real adventure! Count me in!"

Elara smiled, grateful for their support. "Thank you. I'm glad to have you with me."

Dain nodded, his expression thoughtful. "The road to the mountains is treacherous, but if we stick together, I believe we can make it. And who knows? Maybe along the way, we'll find more clues to the mirror's location."

Elara felt a surge of gratitude and relief. She had found her companions, her allies in this journey. Together, they would face whatever challenges lay ahead, and they would do it with courage and determination.

As the night wore on, they continued to talk, sharing stories of their pasts and their hopes for the future. Elara learned that Dain had once been a knight, serving a lord in the northern territories, but had left that life behind after a falling out with his liege. Breck was a blacksmith by trade, though his rough exterior hid a heart of gold. Lyra, it turned out, was a skilled thief, her nimble fingers and sharp mind making her invaluable in situations where stealth and cunning were required. Tomas, the youngest of the group, was an apprentice healer, eager to prove himself in the world.

They were an unlikely group, but as the night deepened and the fire burned low, Elara felt a bond forming between them—a bond forged not by blood, but by shared purpose and a common goal.

When the innkeeper finally announced that it was time to retire for the night, Elara felt a sense of contentment that she had not felt in days. She had found her allies, her companions on this journey, and for the first time since leaving Briar Glen, she felt truly ready to face whatever lay ahead.

The next morning, the group set out at first light, the sun just beginning to peek over the horizon. The air was cool and crisp, filled with the promise of a new day. Elara, Dain, Breck, Lyra, and Tomas walked together, their packs slung over their shoulders, their weapons close at hand. The road ahead was long, but they were ready for it.

As they traveled, Elara found herself growing more comfortable with her new companions. Dain, with his easygoing charm and quick wit, kept the mood light, telling stories of his time as a knight and the many adventures he had experienced since. Breck was quieter, but his steady presence and no-nonsense attitude provided a sense of stability that was reassuring. Lyra, though reserved, had a sharp mind and a keen sense of observation, often pointing out details that the others had missed. Tomas, with his boundless enthusiasm and youthful energy, brought a sense of optimism to the group that was infectious.

They traveled through forests and across fields, the landscape shifting and changing with each passing day. The road was not without its challenges—at times, they encountered treacherous terrain, and more than once they had to fend off bandits or wild animals that threatened their progress. But through it all, they worked together, each using their unique skills to overcome the obstacles they faced.

One evening, as they made camp by the side of the road, Dain approached Elara, his expression serious. "Elara, I've been thinking. The Mirror of Eldoria is said to be hidden in a place of great power, guarded by ancient forces. If we're going to find it, we'll need more than just strength and skill—we'll need knowledge. We need someone who understands the old ways, who can guide us through the challenges we're sure to face."

Elara nodded, understanding his point. "You're right. But where will we find such a person?"

Dain's eyes sparkled with mischief. "I have an idea. There's an old woman who lives in the mountains, not far from here. She's a wise woman, a seer, they say. If anyone can help us, it's her."

Breck, who had been listening from nearby, grunted in agreement. "Aye, I've heard of her. They call her the Witch of the North. Some say she's lived for hundreds of years, that she knows the secrets of the ancient world."

Lyra's expression was skeptical, but she nodded. "It's worth a try. If she can help us, we should seek her out."

Tomas's eyes were wide with excitement. "A real witch? This just keeps getting better!"

Elara smiled at his enthusiasm, though she couldn't help but feel a twinge of apprehension. The idea of seeking out a witch, a woman who was said to possess great power and knowledge, was both thrilling and frightening. But she knew that Dain was right—they needed someone with knowledge of the old ways if they were to succeed in their quest.

"Let's do it," she said, her voice firm. "Let's find the Witch of the North."

The decision made, they packed up their camp the next morning and set off in search of the witch. The journey took them deeper into the mountains, the air growing colder and the landscape more rugged with each passing day. The road became narrow and treacherous, winding its way through steep cliffs and dense forests. But they pressed on, driven by the knowledge that their goal was within reach.

After several days of travel, they finally arrived at the base of a mountain that towered above them, its peak lost in the clouds. At the foot of the mountain stood a small, weathered cabin, its wooden walls covered in moss and ivy. Smoke curled lazily from the chimney, and the scent of herbs and spices filled the air.

"This is it," Dain said, his voice low. "The Witch of the North lives here."

Elara felt a shiver run down her spine as she approached the cabin, her heart pounding with a mixture of excitement and fear. She had come so far, and now she was about to meet the person who might hold the key to finding the Mirror of Eldoria.

Dain stepped forward and knocked on the door, his expression serious. For a moment, there was no response, and Elara wondered if they had come all this way for nothing. But then, the door creaked open, and an old woman appeared in the doorway.

She was small and frail-looking, her back hunched with age, but there was a sharpness in her eyes that belied her appearance. Her hair was a wild tangle of white, and her skin was wrinkled and weathered, like the bark of an ancient tree. She wore a simple dress made of rough-spun wool, and a shawl was draped over her shoulders.

The old woman looked them over, her gaze piercing. "What do you want?" she asked, her voice raspy but strong.

Dain bowed his head respectfully. "We seek your counsel, wise one. We are on a journey to find the Mirror of Eldoria, and we need your guidance."

The old woman's eyes narrowed, and she stepped aside, gesturing for them to enter. "Come in, then. Let's see what you're made of."

Elara and the others exchanged glances, then stepped inside the cabin. The interior was small but cozy, with a fire crackling in the hearth and shelves lined with jars of herbs and potions. A table stood in the center of the room, covered in various trinkets and scrolls, and the air was thick with the scent of incense.

The old woman closed the door behind them and hobbled over to the table, where she took a seat in a worn wooden chair. She gestured for them to sit as well, and they did, feeling slightly out of place in the witch's domain.

The old woman eyed them critically, her gaze lingering on each of them in turn. "So, you seek the Mirror of Eldoria," she said, her voice thoughtful. "Do you even know what you're asking for?"

Elara met her gaze, trying to keep her voice steady. "We know that it is a powerful artifact, one that can reveal one's true destiny. We believe it is hidden in a place of great power, guarded by ancient forces. We need your help to find it."

The old woman chuckled, a dry, rasping sound. "Ah, you're not entirely ignorant, then. That's something." She leaned forward, her eyes gleaming with interest. "But the mirror is not just a tool—it is a test. It shows not only one's destiny, but also one's soul. It will reveal your deepest fears, your darkest secrets, and it will challenge you in ways you cannot imagine. Are you truly prepared for that?"

Elara hesitated, the weight of the witch's words settling heavily on her. But then she nodded, her resolve firm. "Yes. I have to be."

The old woman studied her for a moment longer, then nodded. "Very well. I will help you. But know this—the path you have chosen is fraught with danger. There will be trials, and there will be losses. You must be strong, and you must trust in each other, for only together will you have the strength to succeed."

Elara nodded, her heart pounding with a mixture of fear and determination. "We will."

The old woman reached into a pouch at her side and pulled out a small vial filled with a shimmering liquid. She handed it to Elara, her expression serious. "This is a potion of insight. It will help you see the truth, even when it is hidden. Use it wisely."

Elara took the vial, her fingers trembling slightly. "Thank you."

The old woman nodded, then turned her gaze to the others. "And you, brave knight, cunning thief, steadfast smith, and eager healer—you each have a role to play in this journey. Trust in your strengths, and do not fear the darkness. For even in the darkest of places, there is light to be found."

Dain, Breck, Lyra, and Tomas all nodded, their expressions serious. They knew that the road ahead would be difficult, but they were ready to face it together.

The old woman leaned back in her chair, her eyes closing as if in thought. "You will find the entrance to the mirror's domain in the Valley of Shadows, beyond the Blackwood Forest. But beware—the forest is alive with ancient magic, and it will not let you pass easily. You must prove your worth, or you will be lost to the shadows forever."

Elara's heart skipped a beat. The Valley of Shadows—the name alone sent a chill down her spine. But she knew that this was the path she had to take, no matter how dangerous it might be.

"Thank you," she said, her voice firm. "We won't let you down."

The old woman's eyes opened, and she gave Elara a small, knowing smile. "We shall see, child. We shall see."

With that, she stood and gestured for them to leave. "Go now, and may the spirits guide you on your journey. But remember—strength alone will not see you through. You must also have courage, wisdom, and heart."

Elara and the others stood and made their way to the door, their hearts heavy with the knowledge of what lay ahead. But as they stepped out into the cold mountain air, they felt a sense of purpose, a determination to see their quest through to the end.

As they made their way back down the mountain, Elara felt a strange sense of peace settle over her. She had her allies, her companions in this journey, and she knew that together, they could face whatever challenges lay ahead. The road would be difficult, and there would be dangers and trials that would test them to their limits. But with each other's support, they could overcome anything.

The sun was setting as they reached the base of the mountain, casting long shadows over the land. Elara looked out at the landscape before them, the rolling hills and dense forests bathed in the warm glow of the evening light.

"We're ready," she said softly, more to herself than to the others. "We're ready for whatever comes next."

Dain, who had been walking beside her, nodded. "Aye. We are."

Breck, Lyra, and Tomas all voiced their agreement, their expressions resolute. They were a band of unlikely companions, brought together by fate and bound by a shared purpose. And as they set off toward the Valley of Shadows, they knew that they were more than just travelers—they were a team, united in their quest to find the Mirror of Eldoria.

The journey ahead would be long and difficult, but they were ready. And as they walked into the twilight, the stars beginning to twinkle in the darkening sky, Elara felt a spark of hope ignite within her.

For she knew that they were not just searching for a mirror—they were searching for themselves, for the truth that lay hidden within each of them. And no matter what trials they faced, they would face them together.

End of Chapter 3.

Chapter 4: The First Trial: The Forest of Whispers

The sun dipped below the horizon, casting long shadows across the landscape as Elara and her companions stood at the edge of the Forest of Whispers. The sky, painted in hues of orange and pink, gave way to the encroaching darkness that seemed to bleed out from the forest itself, a darkness deeper than night, as if the very trees exhaled a fog of gloom and uncertainty. The forest loomed before them, its trees twisted and gnarled, their branches reaching out like skeletal fingers against the dimming sky. The air was thick and heavy, almost suffocating, and the sound of rustling leaves was unnervingly loud in the silence.

For a long moment, none of them spoke. The weight of the task before them—the first real test of their journey—hung heavily in the air. Elara could feel her heart pounding in her chest, the pulse of her anxiety matching the rhythm of her breath. This was no ordinary forest; it was a place of legend, a place where the line between reality and illusion blurred, where even the bravest souls could lose themselves to the darkness within.

Dain was the first to break the silence. The former knight's usually confident demeanor was strained, his eyes narrowed as he studied the treeline. "The Forest of Whispers," he said, his voice low and steady. "I've heard stories about this place. They say the forest speaks to you, shows you things—your deepest fears, your darkest memories. It's a place of illusions, meant to lead travelers astray."

Lyra, the thief, glanced at Dain, her sharp eyes scanning the treeline for any signs of danger. "I've heard those stories too," she said, her voice just above a whisper. "But they also say there's a path through the forest, a true path. If you can find it, you can make it to the other side. But if you lose your way..."

She let the sentence hang in the air, unfinished but clear. If you lose your way, you may never find it again.

Breck, the blacksmith, grunted in agreement. "The path will be hard to find, and the forest will do everything it can to keep us from it. We'll need to stay close, trust each other, and not let the illusions get into our heads."

Tomas, the healer's apprentice, shifted nervously from foot to foot, his wide eyes fixed on the darkness ahead. "But how will we know what's real and what isn't? If the forest can show us anything, how can we trust what we see?"

Elara took a deep breath, steadying herself. She could feel the tension in the group, the uncertainty that gnawed at each of them. This was their first true test as a team, and it would require more than just strength or skill. It would require trust—trust in each other and in themselves.

"We have to rely on each other," Elara said, her voice stronger than she felt. "We've come this far together, and we've faced challenges already. This is just another one. If we stay close, keep our minds clear, and trust in each other, we can find the true path and make it through."

Dain nodded, his expression resolute. "Elara's right. We've faced dangers before, and we'll face them again. But we're stronger together. Whatever the forest throws at us, we'll face it as a team."

Breck and Lyra nodded in agreement, their expressions serious. Tomas still looked nervous, but he swallowed hard and nodded as well. "I'm with you," he said, though his voice wavered slightly.

Elara smiled at him, hoping to give him some reassurance. "We'll be okay, Tomas. We'll get through this."

With a final, steadying breath, Elara turned toward the forest, her heart pounding in her chest. The trees loomed ahead, their twisted forms almost seeming to shift and move in the fading light. She took a step forward, her companions close behind her, and together they entered the Forest of Whispers.

The moment they crossed the threshold, the atmosphere changed. The air grew colder, the light dimmer, and the sounds of the outside world faded into a muffled silence. The trees towered above them, their branches interwoven to form a thick canopy that blocked out what little light remained. The ground beneath their feet was uneven, the roots of the ancient trees twisting up like the fingers of some buried giant, threatening to trip them with every step.

The forest was alive with sound, though not the kind one would expect from a place of nature. There was no rustling of small animals in the underbrush, no birdsong to lighten the oppressive air. Instead, there was a low murmur, like the susurration of many voices just out of earshot, whispering words that could not be understood. The whispers seemed to come from everywhere at once, surrounding them, pressing in on their minds with a quiet, insistent force.

Elara tried to focus on the path ahead, but the whispers tugged at her thoughts, filling her with unease. It was as if the forest itself was speaking to her, probing the edges of her mind, searching for weaknesses, for fears it could exploit. She forced herself to keep walking, one step at a time, determined not to let the forest get the better of her.

The others were silent, their faces tense and drawn as they followed behind her. Even Dain, usually so quick to crack a joke or offer a reassuring smile, was grim-faced, his eyes darting from shadow to shadow, as if expecting an attack at any moment.

As they moved deeper into the forest, the whispers grew louder, more insistent. The words were still unintelligible, but the tone was unmistakable—taunting, mocking, filled with malice. The forest was testing them, probing their defenses, trying to find a way inside their minds.

Suddenly, the ground beneath them shifted, and Elara stumbled, nearly losing her footing. She reached out to steady herself against a tree, but the moment her hand touched the rough bark, she felt a sharp jolt of fear shoot through her, as if the tree itself had reached into her mind and pulled out one of her deepest, darkest memories.

She gasped, jerking her hand away from the tree as the memory flooded her mind—her mother's death, the overwhelming grief, the sense of loss that had consumed her as a child. She had buried those feelings deep within her, had forced herself to move on, to be strong for her father. But now, the forest had brought them back to the surface, raw and painful, as if no time had passed at all.

"Elara!" Dain's voice broke through the haze of memory, and she blinked, shaking her head to clear it. He was at her side, his hand on her arm, concern etched on his face. "Are you okay?"

Elara took a shaky breath, nodding as she tried to push the memory back down, to regain control. "I'm... I'm fine," she said, though her voice trembled. "The forest... it's trying to get inside our heads. We need to be careful."

Dain nodded, his expression serious. "Stay close," he said, glancing back at the others. "We can't let the forest divide us. If we start to lose our way, if anyone starts to feel overwhelmed, speak up. We have to stay together."

Breck and Lyra nodded, their expressions grim. Tomas looked pale, his eyes wide with fear, but he swallowed hard and nodded as well. "I'm okay," he said, though his voice was barely above a whisper. "I can do this."

Elara forced herself to smile, though it felt strained. "We all can. We just need to keep moving."

They pressed on, each step feeling heavier than the last as the forest closed in around them. The whispers grew louder, more distinct, the words now clear and biting.

"Failure..."

"Lost..."

"Worthless..."

The voices taunted them, each word like a knife to the heart, cutting through their resolve. Elara felt the fear rising within her, the doubts that had always lurked at the edges of her mind now roaring to life, fed by the malevolent presence of the forest. She had always struggled with self-doubt, with the fear that she wasn't strong enough, wasn't worthy of the destiny that had been thrust upon her. And now the forest was using those fears against her, trying to break her will, to make her lose her way.

She glanced at her companions, and she could see that they were struggling too. Dain's jaw was clenched, his hands gripping the hilt of his sword as if it were a lifeline. Breck's face was set in a deep scowl, his eyes narrowed in concentration. Lyra's usually sharp and focused gaze was clouded, her steps unsteady. And Tomas... Tomas looked as if he were barely holding on, his breaths coming in quick, shallow gasps, his hands trembling.

Elara knew they couldn't go on like this. The forest was wearing them down, breaking their spirits, and if they didn't do something soon, they would lose their way—and possibly their lives.

"We need to stop," Elara said, her voice firmer than she felt. "We need to regroup, to clear our minds. The forest is trying to break us, and we can't let it."

Dain nodded, though his expression was strained. "You're right. We need to take a moment, to remind ourselves why we're here, what we're fighting for."

They found a small clearing, barely large enough for them all to sit, and settled down, forming a tight circle. The whispers continued to swirl around them, but Elara forced herself to focus on the faces of her companions, to draw strength from the fact that they were still together, still fighting.

"We can't let the forest get to us," she said, her voice steady. "It's trying to tear us apart, to make us doubt ourselves and each other. But we're stronger than that. We've come this far, and we'll get through this, but only if we stick together."

Breck grunted in agreement, his expression fierce. "Aye, we've faced worse than this. We just need to keep our heads clear, to remember what's real and what's not."

Lyra nodded, though her eyes were still haunted. "We have to trust each other. The forest will try to show us things, to make us doubt. But we can't give in to it."

Tomas, still trembling, looked at each of them in turn, his fear palpable. "I... I'm scared," he admitted, his voice barely above a whisper. "I don't know if I can do this."

Elara reached out, placing a hand on his shoulder, her touch gentle but firm. "You can, Tomas. We all can. But we have to do it together. You're not alone in this."

Tomas looked at her, his eyes wide and vulnerable, but then he nodded, his lips pressed into a thin line of determination. "Okay," he said, his voice a little stronger. "Okay. We can do this."

Elara smiled at him, then turned her gaze to the others. "We're in this together," she said, her voice filled with resolve. "No matter what the forest shows us, no matter what it says, we have to trust each other, to trust that we can make it through. And we will."

Dain nodded, his expression resolute. "We will."

With renewed determination, they stood and continued their journey, the forest closing in around them once more. The whispers continued to plague them, the voices growing louder and more vicious, but they held fast, refusing to let the forest break their resolve.

As they moved deeper into the forest, the ground became more treacherous, the roots of the trees rising up like serpents, threatening to trip them at every turn. The path, which had been difficult to discern from the start, now seemed to vanish entirely, leaving them to navigate by instinct and intuition alone.

The whispers grew more insidious, the voices now taking on the tones of people they knew, people they had loved and lost. Elara heard her mother's voice, soft and sorrowful, reminding her of the day she had died, of the pain and guilt that had consumed her. She heard her father's voice, filled with doubt, questioning whether she was truly capable of fulfilling the prophecy, of finding the Mirror of Eldoria.

Dain heard the voice of his former liege, the lord he had once served with unwavering loyalty, only to be betrayed and cast aside. The voice taunted him, reminding him of his failure, of the disgrace that had driven him to leave everything behind. Breck heard the voice of his father, a stern and unforgiving man who had never believed in him, who had always seen him as a disappointment. Lyra heard the voice of her sister, the only family she had ever known, who had turned on her, betraying her trust and leaving her to fend for herself on the streets. And Tomas... Tomas heard the voice of his mentor, the healer who had taken him in, who had tried to teach him the ways of healing, only to be lost to a disease Tomas had been unable to cure.

The voices were relentless, tearing at their hearts, filling them with doubt and despair. But even as the forest tried to break them, they held on to each other, drawing strength from their shared determination to see their journey through to the end.

They continued on, step by painful step, until they reached a fork in the path, two trails leading off into the darkness. The whispers grew louder, more chaotic, as if the forest itself were trying to push them in different directions, to separate them from each other.

Elara stared at the two paths, her heart pounding with indecision. She knew that choosing the wrong path could be disastrous, that they could be lost forever in the forest's depths. But the whispers made it impossible to think clearly, to discern which path was the true one.

"We have to choose," Dain said, his voice strained. "But which one?"

Lyra narrowed her eyes, her expression thoughtful. "The forest is trying to confuse us, to make us doubt ourselves. We have to trust our instincts, to trust each other."

Elara closed her eyes, trying to block out the whispers, to clear her mind. She took a deep breath, focusing on the warmth in her chest, the same warmth she had felt when she had first accepted her destiny. She let that warmth guide her, let it lead her to the path that felt right.

When she opened her eyes, she pointed to the path on the left. "This way," she said, her voice firm. "This is the true path."

The others looked at her, their expressions a mix of doubt and trust. But they had come this far together, and they knew that they had to rely on each other if they were to succeed.

With a final nod of agreement, they took the path Elara had chosen, the whispers still echoing in their minds, but their resolve unbroken.

The path was narrow and winding, the trees pressing in close on either side. The whispers continued to taunt them, the voices of their loved ones growing louder, more insistent, as if trying to pull them back, to make them turn around and abandon their journey. But they pressed on, refusing to give in to the forest's tricks.

As they moved deeper into the forest, the path began to change, the ground becoming softer, almost spongy beneath their feet. The air grew thicker, the darkness more oppressive, until it felt as if they were walking through a tunnel of shadows, the light from the outside world completely cut off.

But then, just as the darkness seemed unbearable, they saw a faint light ahead, a glimmer of hope in the distance. They quickened their pace, their hearts pounding with anticipation, and as they drew closer, the light grew brighter, until they stepped out into a clearing bathed in a soft, ethereal glow.

The clearing was small, surrounded on all sides by the towering trees of the forest, but the air was different here—lighter, clearer, as if the oppressive weight of the forest had lifted. In the center of the clearing stood a single tree, its branches twisted and gnarled, but its leaves a vibrant green, glowing with a soft, otherworldly light.

Elara approached the tree, her heart pounding with a mix of awe and relief. She could feel the warmth in her chest growing stronger, the same warmth that had guided her through the forest, that had led her to this place. She knew, with a certainty that went beyond words, that this was the true path, that they had found the heart of the Forest of Whispers.

The others joined her, their expressions filled with wonder and relief. The whispers had faded, the voices silenced, and for the first time since entering the forest, they could think clearly, could breathe freely.

"This is it," Dain said, his voice filled with reverence. "We found the true path."

Elara nodded, her heart swelling with pride and gratitude. They had done it—they had faced the forest's illusions, had overcome their fears and doubts, and had found the way through.

But even as they stood there, basking in their victory, Elara knew that this was only the first of many trials they would face. The journey ahead would be long and difficult, filled with challenges that would test them in ways they could not yet imagine. But she also knew that they were stronger now, that they had proven to themselves and to each other that they could face whatever lay ahead.

As they left the clearing and continued on their journey, the light of the clearing fading behind them, Elara felt a sense of hope and determination settle over her. They had faced the darkness of the forest and had come out stronger, more united than ever before.

And as they walked into the unknown, she knew that, together, they could overcome any trial that awaited them.

End of Chapter 4.

Chapter 5: The Cursed Village

The days following their escape from the Forest of Whispers were spent in a wary silence as Elara and her companions traveled eastward. The memory of their trial in the forest lingered like a shadow over their thoughts, a reminder of the dangers that lay ahead. Each step felt heavier than the last as they moved through the rugged landscape, the path ahead growing more treacherous with every mile.

The terrain shifted from the dense, twisted woods of the Forest of Whispers to a barren, rocky expanse. The ground was cracked and dry, the air thick with dust and the scent of decay. The once vibrant foliage was replaced by jagged cliffs and crumbling earth, the landscape as desolate and unforgiving as the journey that lay before them.

As the group pushed forward, the sun hung low in the sky, casting an orange glow over the desolate land. The day had been long, and they had yet to find any sign of shelter. Their provisions were running low, and the prospect of another night in the open, exposed to the elements, weighed heavily on their minds.

"I don't like this place," Tomas muttered, his voice tinged with unease as he looked around the barren landscape. The young healer's apprentice had grown quieter since their trial in the forest, his usual optimism dulled by the harsh realities of their journey.

Breck, the blacksmith, grunted in agreement, his eyes scanning the horizon for any signs of danger. "Aye, this land is cursed," he said, his voice low and grim. "There's nothing here but death and despair. We need to find shelter before night falls."

Lyra, the thief, pulled her cloak tighter around her, her sharp eyes narrowed against the dust-filled wind that whipped across the barren ground. "We've been walking for hours," she said, her tone clipped. "There's no shelter to be found here."

Dain, ever the pragmatist, glanced at the sky, noting the way the light was beginning to fade. "We need to keep moving," he said, his voice steady. "There has to be something ahead—a cave, an outcropping, anything that can provide cover."

Elara nodded, though her own spirits were beginning to wane. The landscape seemed to stretch on forever, an endless expanse of rock and dust with no end in sight. But they couldn't afford to stop, not when night was so close. They had to keep moving, had to find shelter before the darkness claimed them.

As they pressed on, the wind began to pick up, howling through the rocky terrain with a mournful wail. The sky above them darkened, the fading light of the sun swallowed by thick, heavy clouds that seemed to hang low over the earth. The air grew colder, the temperature dropping rapidly as the last remnants of daylight slipped away.

The darkness came quickly, faster than any of them had anticipated. One moment they were walking in the dim light of dusk, and the next they were plunged into a deep, impenetrable night. The wind howled around them, whipping at their cloaks and filling the air with a fine, choking dust that stung their eyes and filled their lungs.

"We need to stop!" Tomas shouted over the wind, his voice barely audible above the gale. "We can't see anything in this darkness!"

Elara knew he was right. They were effectively blind in the pitch black, stumbling over rocks and loose earth with every step. But the thought of stopping, of being exposed to the elements with no shelter, filled her with dread.

"We have to find cover!" she shouted back, her voice hoarse from the dust. "There has to be something—"

Her words were cut off as the ground beneath her gave way. With a gasp, she felt herself falling, the rocky earth crumbling beneath her feet. She reached out, trying to grab hold of something—anything—to stop her fall, but her hands found only empty air.

"Elara!" Dain's voice rang out in the darkness, filled with alarm.

But before she could call out in response, she hit the ground hard, the impact driving the breath from her lungs. Pain shot through her as she landed in a heap, her body jarred by the fall. She lay there for a moment, stunned, her mind struggling to process what had just happened.

"Elara, are you okay?" Dain's voice was closer now, filled with concern.

Elara groaned, pushing herself up onto her hands and knees. "I'm... I'm okay," she managed, though her body ached from the impact. "Just... just give me a moment."

The darkness was absolute, so thick that she couldn't see her own hand in front of her face. She could hear the others scrambling to find their way down to her, their voices muffled by the howling wind.

"Elara, where are you?" Lyra's voice called out, her tone urgent.

"I'm here," Elara replied, though her voice was weak. "I'm—"

Before she could finish her sentence, she felt a hand on her arm, helping her to her feet. It was Dain, his presence a steadying force in the chaos of the night.

"Thank the gods," he muttered, his grip firm as he supported her. "Are you hurt?"

Elara shook her head, though the motion made her dizzy. "I'm fine," she said, trying to steady herself. "Just a bit shaken."

The others soon joined them, their faces pale and drawn in the dim light of the lantern that Tomas had managed to light. The small flame flickered weakly in the wind, casting long shadows on the rocky ground around them.

"What happened?" Breck asked, his voice gruff with concern.

"I fell," Elara explained, her voice still shaky. "The ground gave way. I didn't see it in the dark."

Lyra's sharp eyes scanned the area, taking in the rocky terrain around them. "This is bad," she said, her tone clipped. "We can't stay out here. The wind's picking up, and it's only going to get worse."

Dain nodded, his expression grim. "We need to find shelter, and fast. Elara, can you walk?"

Elara nodded, though her legs still felt unsteady beneath her. "Yes, I'm fine. Let's keep moving."

With the faint light of the lantern guiding their way, they pressed on through the darkness, the wind howling around them like a pack of hungry wolves. The ground was treacherous, the rocks loose and uneven, and every step felt like a struggle against the elements.

But then, just as despair was beginning to take hold, Lyra called out, her voice filled with relief. "There—look!"

Elara squinted into the darkness, trying to see what Lyra had spotted. And then she saw it—a faint glow in the distance, just beyond the ridge of a rocky hill. It was the soft, warm light of a fire, flickering in the night like a beacon of hope.

"Thank the gods," Dain muttered, his voice filled with relief. "That has to be a village or camp. Let's move."

With renewed determination, they made their way toward the light, each step bringing them closer to the promise of shelter and warmth. As they crested the ridge, the source of the light came into view—a small village nestled in a narrow valley, its stone buildings huddled together as if for warmth against the cold night.

The village was unlike any they had seen before. The buildings were old and weathered, their stone walls cracked and crumbling with age. The streets were narrow and winding, lined with cobblestones that were slick with moisture. And the light—there was no sun or moon to cast it, only a strange, eerie glow that seemed to emanate from the very stones of the village itself.

As they descended into the valley, the wind began to die down, the howling gale reduced to a low, mournful wail that echoed through the narrow streets. The air grew colder, the chill seeping into their bones as they approached the village.

"There's something not right about this place," Breck muttered, his eyes narrowed as he scanned the darkened windows of the buildings. "It feels... wrong."

Elara couldn't help but agree. There was an unnatural stillness to the village, as if the very air was holding its breath, waiting for something to happen. The light that bathed the streets was too soft, too diffuse, casting long shadows that seemed to move on their own.

But there was no turning back now. They had come too far, and they needed shelter. With a deep breath, Elara led the way into the village, her senses on high alert.

The streets were deserted, the only sound the soft crunch of their footsteps on the cobblestones. The buildings loomed above them, their windows dark and empty, like the hollow eyes of a skull. The eerie light cast everything in a strange, otherworldly glow, making it difficult to discern where the shadows ended and the light began.

As they moved deeper into the village, a sense of unease settled over them, growing stronger with each step. Elara could feel it too—a weight in the air, a pressure that seemed to press down on them from all sides.

"We need to find someone," Dain said, his voice tense. "There has to be someone here who can tell us what's going on."

But the village remained silent, its streets empty and its windows dark. There was no sign of life, no movement, no sound other than the faint whisper of the wind.

Elara's heart began to pound in her chest, a sense of dread creeping up her spine. Something was wrong here—terribly, horribly wrong.

Suddenly, a door creaked open nearby, the sound loud in the silence. The group froze, their eyes snapping to the source of the noise.

A figure emerged from the shadows, stepping out of the doorway and into the eerie light. It was an old man, his back hunched with age, his face lined with deep wrinkles. He wore a tattered cloak that hung loosely around his frail frame, and his eyes were wide and fearful as he looked at them.

"Strangers," he croaked, his voice raspy and weak. "What are you doing here?"

Elara stepped forward, her heart pounding. "We're travelers," she said, trying to keep her voice steady. "We were caught in the storm, and we need shelter. Can you help us?"

The old man's eyes widened even further, and he shook his head, his expression one of terror. "You shouldn't have come here," he whispered, his voice trembling. "This place... it's cursed. The night... it never ends."

Elara felt a chill run down her spine. "What do you mean?"

The old man glanced around nervously, as if afraid of being overheard. "The sorcerer," he said, his voice barely above a whisper. "He cursed this village, trapped us in eternal night. The sun never rises here, and we're doomed to live in darkness forever."

Elara's breath caught in her throat. "A sorcerer? Why would he do this?"

The old man shook his head, his expression one of despair. "I don't know. No one knows. But he's powerful—too powerful. We've tried to fight him, to lift the curse, but it's no use. We're trapped here, forever."

Dain stepped forward, his expression grim. "Where can we find this sorcerer?"

The old man's eyes widened in horror. "No, you can't! He'll destroy you, just like he destroyed us!"

But Elara knew they had no choice. The sorcerer held the key to lifting the curse, and possibly to finding the Mirror of Eldoria. They had to confront him, no matter the cost.

"Please," she said, her voice firm but gentle. "We have to try. We have to lift this curse."

The old man stared at her for a long moment, his expression filled with a mix of fear and hope. Finally, he nodded, though his eyes were filled with sorrow. "He lives in the tower at the edge of the village," he said, his voice trembling. "But be careful—he's not like any man you've ever faced. He's... something else."

Elara nodded, her heart pounding with a mixture of fear and determination. "Thank you."

The old man turned and shuffled back into his house, the door closing behind him with a final, ominous creak.

The group stood in silence for a moment, the weight of the task ahead pressing down on them like a physical force. The tower loomed in the distance, its dark silhouette barely visible against the night sky.

"This is it," Dain said, his voice steady but tense. "We have to confront the sorcerer and lift this curse."

Lyra nodded, her sharp eyes narrowed in determination. "We can't let fear stop us. We've come too far."

Breck grunted in agreement, his hands tightening on the hilt of his hammer. "Let's get this over with."

Tomas, though still pale and trembling, nodded as well. "We can do this," he said, though his voice wavered slightly. "We have to."

Elara took a deep breath, steeling herself for the challenge ahead. The tower loomed before them, a dark and foreboding presence that seemed to pulse with malevolent energy. But they had no choice. If they were to find the Mirror of Eldoria, they had to face the sorcerer and lift the curse.

With a final nod to her companions, Elara led the way toward the tower, her heart pounding with fear and resolve. The path was narrow and winding, the stones beneath their feet slick with moisture. The wind had died down, leaving an eerie silence in its wake, broken only by the soft crunch of their footsteps on the cobblestones.

As they approached the tower, the sense of dread grew stronger, the air thickening with a palpable tension. The tower itself was ancient, its stone walls cracked and weathered with age. Vines and ivy clung to its surface, twisting around the darkened windows like the fingers of some unseen force.

The door to the tower was massive, made of heavy oak and reinforced with iron bands. It stood slightly ajar, a thin sliver of light visible through the crack. Elara hesitated for a moment, her hand hovering over the door, before steeling herself and pushing it open.

The door creaked loudly as it swung inward, revealing a dimly lit chamber beyond. The air inside was cold and damp, filled with the scent of dust and decay. The walls were lined with shelves cluttered with strange artifacts and ancient tomes, the floor covered in a thick layer of dust that muffled their footsteps.

At the far end of the chamber, a figure stood in the shadows, shrouded in darkness. The sorcerer.

Elara's heart pounded in her chest as she stepped forward, her companions close behind her. The sorcerer remained still, his presence a dark and oppressive force that filled the room.

"So, you've come to confront me," the sorcerer said, his voice low and resonant, echoing off the stone walls. "Foolish. You cannot hope to defeat me."

Elara took a deep breath, forcing herself to remain calm. "We're here to lift the curse you've placed on this village," she said, her voice steady. "Why have you done this? What do you hope to gain?"

The sorcerer chuckled, a dark, mirthless sound that sent a shiver down her spine. "The villagers were fools. They defied me, refused to give me what I wanted. So, I took what was mine. I trapped them in eternal night, a fitting punishment for their insolence."

Elara's fists clenched at her sides, anger flaring within her. "And what is it that you wanted? What could they have done to deserve this?"

The sorcerer stepped forward, his form emerging from the shadows. He was tall and thin, his skin pale and almost translucent, his eyes glowing with an unnatural light. His robes were tattered and worn, the fabric swirling around him like smoke.

"What I wanted," the sorcerer said, his voice dripping with contempt, "was the mirror. The Mirror of Eldoria."

Elara's breath caught in her throat. "The mirror? You know where it is?"

The sorcerer smiled, a cruel, twisted expression that sent a chill down her spine. "I know where it is," he said, his voice filled with dark amusement. "But you will never find it. The mirror is hidden, protected by powerful magic that only I can break. And I have no intention of doing so."

Elara's mind raced, trying to find a way to reason with him. "What do you want with the mirror?" she asked, her voice steady despite the fear gnawing at her insides. "Why is it so important to you?"

The sorcerer's eyes narrowed, his expression darkening. "The mirror holds great power—power that should belong to me. With it, I could control my destiny, shape the world to my will. But the villagers... they refused to give it to me. They hid it from me, thinking they could defy me. So, I cursed them. I cursed them to live in eternal night, to suffer for their defiance."

Elara took a step forward, her heart pounding with resolve. "But you can still break the curse," she said, her voice firm. "You can still lift it and let the villagers go free."

The sorcerer laughed, a harsh, grating sound that echoed through the chamber. "And why would I do that? What could you possibly offer me that would make me lift the curse?"

Elara's mind raced, trying to find something—anything—that could convince him. But before she could speak, Dain stepped forward, his expression determined.

"What if we find the mirror for you?" Dain said, his voice steady. "If you break the curse and let the villagers go free, we'll help you find the mirror."

Elara's heart skipped a beat. She hadn't expected Dain to make such an offer, but as she thought about it, she realized it might be their only chance.

The sorcerer's eyes gleamed with interest. "And why would I trust you? How do I know you won't betray me?"

Dain met the sorcerer's gaze without flinching. "You don't," he said simply. "But if you don't lift the curse, the villagers will continue to suffer. And without us, you might never find the mirror. This is your best chance."

The sorcerer was silent for a long moment, his glowing eyes studying them intently. Elara could feel the tension in the air, the weight of the decision hanging over them like a sword.

Finally, the sorcerer nodded, a slow, deliberate motion. "Very well," he said, his voice filled with dark satisfaction. "I will lift the curse—but only if you bring me the mirror. If you fail, the curse will return, and the villagers will suffer even more."

Elara nodded, relief flooding through her. "We'll do it. We'll find the mirror and bring it to you."

The sorcerer smiled, a cold, calculating expression that sent a shiver down her spine. "Good," he said, his voice soft and dangerous. "But remember—if you fail, the curse will return, and it will be worse than before. Do not think you can deceive me."

With that, the sorcerer raised his hands, his long fingers moving through the air as he began to chant in a language Elara didn't understand. The air around them seemed to vibrate with energy, a dark, oppressive force that pressed down on them like a physical weight.

And then, with a final, powerful word, the sorcerer lowered his hands, and the oppressive darkness that had hung over the village began to lift. The heavy clouds above them parted, allowing the faint light of the moon to shine down on the village for the first time in what felt like an eternity.

The villagers, who had been hiding in their homes, began to emerge, their eyes wide with wonder as they looked up at the sky. The curse had been lifted, if only temporarily.

Elara turned to the sorcerer, her heart pounding with a mix of fear and resolve. "We'll find the mirror," she said, her voice firm. "And when we do, we'll bring it to you."

The sorcerer nodded, his glowing eyes filled with dark satisfaction. "See that you do," he said, his voice low and threatening. "Or the villagers will pay the price."

With that, the sorcerer turned and vanished into the shadows, leaving Elara and her companions alone in the chamber.

For a long moment, they stood in silence, the weight of the task ahead pressing down on them like a heavy burden. The curse had been lifted, but only temporarily. They had to find the Mirror of Eldoria—and they had to do it quickly, before the sorcerer's wrath returned.

"We have to move fast," Dain said, his voice tense. "The sorcerer won't give us much time."

Elara nodded, her mind racing. "We need to find the mirror—and we need to find it soon. The villagers are counting on us."

Breck grunted in agreement, his expression grim. "Let's get moving."

With renewed determination, they left the tower and made their way back into the village, the faint light of the moon guiding their way. The villagers, still in awe of the lifted curse, watched them with wide, hopeful eyes, their expressions filled with a mix of gratitude and fear.

Elara felt a surge of responsibility as she looked at them. These people had suffered for so long, trapped in eternal night by the sorcerer's curse. They were counting on her and her companions to find the mirror and lift the curse for good.

"We'll find it," she murmured to herself, her voice filled with resolve. "We have to."

As they left the village and made their way into the night, Elara felt a strange sense of hope and determination settle over her. The journey ahead would be long and difficult, filled with challenges that would test them in ways they could not yet imagine. But with each other's support, they could overcome anything.

They had faced the darkness of the Forest of Whispers, had confronted the sorcerer and lifted the curse, if only temporarily. And now, they were closer than ever to finding the Mirror of Eldoria.

The night was cold and the path ahead uncertain, but Elara knew they were ready for whatever lay ahead. Together, they would find the mirror, lift the curse, and fulfill their destiny.

End of Chapter 5.

Chapter 6: The River of Reflection

The air was crisp and cool as Elara and her companions left the cursed village behind, the faint glow of dawn just beginning to touch the horizon. They had spent the night in the village, taking refuge in the temporary reprieve from the eternal darkness that had plagued the land for so long. The villagers, now free from the oppressive curse, had thanked them profusely, their relief palpable. But Elara knew their work was far from over. The sorcerer's curse had been lifted, but only temporarily. If they failed to find the Mirror of Eldoria and deliver it to the sorcerer, the villagers would be plunged back into eternal night, their suffering even greater than before.

With this knowledge weighing heavily on her mind, Elara led the way as they traveled eastward, their path taking them through a dense forest that gradually gave way to rolling hills and open plains. The sun was rising steadily now, its golden light casting long shadows across the landscape. The world seemed to be waking up around them, the air filled with the sounds of birdsong and the rustling of leaves in the gentle breeze.

But despite the beauty of the morning, Elara couldn't shake the sense of unease that had settled over her since their encounter with the sorcerer. The task ahead of them was daunting, and the weight of responsibility felt almost unbearable. They had to find the Mirror of Eldoria—not just to lift the curse, but to fulfill the prophecy that had brought them together in the first place. The fate of the kingdom rested on their shoulders, and the path ahead was fraught with danger and uncertainty.

As they traveled, the landscape began to change once more. The rolling hills flattened out, giving way to a vast, open plain that stretched out as far as the eye could see. The grass was tall and golden, waving gently in the breeze like a sea of gold. In the distance, Elara could see a dark line on the horizon, a band of shadow that seemed to cut through the golden plains like a scar.

"That must be the River of Reflection," Dain said, his voice low and thoughtful as he followed her gaze.

Elara nodded, her heart beginning to race. The River of Reflection was a place of legend, a magical river that was said to show travelers visions of their past—visions that could reveal their deepest fears, regrets, and desires. It was a place of great power, but also great danger. Many who had sought the river's waters had never returned, lost to the visions that consumed them.

"We need to be careful," she said, her voice steady but filled with a sense of foreboding. "The river shows you things—things you might not want to see. We have to be prepared for whatever it reveals."

Lyra, the thief, nodded, her sharp eyes narrowing as she studied the distant line of shadow. "I've heard stories about the River of Reflection," she said, her voice thoughtful. "They say it shows you the truth, whether you're ready to face it or not."

Breck, the blacksmith, grunted in agreement. "Aye, but it also shows you your past—the things you've done, the mistakes you've made. It can be a cruel mirror, reflecting all the things you'd rather forget."

Tomas, the healer's apprentice, looked uneasy, his eyes wide with a mix of fear and curiosity. "Do we really have to cross it?" he asked, his voice trembling slightly. "Is there no other way?"

Elara shook her head, her expression grim. "This is the path we have to take. The river is part of our journey—part of the trials we must face if we're going to find the mirror. We can't avoid it."

Tomas swallowed hard, but he nodded, his resolve firming. "I understand. I'll do my best."

With that, they continued on, their pace steady but cautious as they approached the river. The closer they got, the more Elara could feel the tension building within her, a tight knot of anxiety that seemed to coil in her chest. She knew that the river would reveal things about herself that she might not be ready to face—things she had buried deep within her, hidden away in the darkest corners of her mind. But she also knew that this was a test she had to pass, a trial she had to endure if she was to fulfill her destiny.

As they neared the river, the golden grass gave way to a barren, rocky landscape. The ground was hard and uneven, the rocks jagged and sharp underfoot. The air grew colder, the warmth of the sun barely penetrating the heavy mist that seemed to rise from the river itself. The once bright and open sky was now shrouded in a thick, swirling fog that obscured the horizon, leaving only the dark, murky waters of the river visible.

The River of Reflection stretched out before them, its waters dark and still, like a mirror reflecting the gloomy sky above. The river was wide and slow-moving, its surface as smooth as glass, with only the occasional ripple disturbing its calm. The mist clung to the water like a shroud, swirling in ghostly tendrils that reached out toward the shore, as if beckoning them closer.

Elara felt a shiver run down her spine as she approached the riverbank, the knot of anxiety tightening in her chest. The air was thick with the scent of damp earth and decaying leaves, the atmosphere heavy with a sense of foreboding. She could feel the magic of the river, a powerful and ancient force that seemed to hum just beneath the surface of the water, waiting to be awakened.

"This is it," Dain said, his voice low and tense as he stood beside her. "The River of Reflection."

Elara nodded, her gaze fixed on the dark waters before them. "We have to cross it," she said, her voice steady but filled with a sense of dread. "But be careful. The river will show you things—things you might not want to see. We have to stay focused, stay together."

Lyra, ever the pragmatist, stepped forward, her sharp eyes scanning the riverbank. "We'll need to find a way across," she said, her tone thoughtful. "The river's too wide to swim, and the current's too strong. There has to be a bridge or a crossing point somewhere."

Breck nodded, his gaze fixed on the distant shore. "We'll need to move quickly. The longer we stay here, the more the river's magic will affect us."

Tomas looked pale, his hands trembling slightly as he gripped his staff. "I'm ready," he said, though his voice wavered. "I'll do my best."

Elara took a deep breath, steeling herself for what was to come. She knew that the river's magic would be powerful, that it would test them in ways they could not yet imagine. But she also knew that this was a trial they had to face, a necessary step on their journey to find the Mirror of Eldoria.

With a final nod to her companions, Elara led the way along the riverbank, her eyes scanning the fog-shrouded waters for any sign of a crossing. The air was thick with tension, the silence oppressive, broken only by the soft rustle of their footsteps on the rocky ground.

As they walked, the mist seemed to grow thicker, swirling around them like a living thing. The air grew colder, the temperature dropping rapidly as the fog closed in, obscuring the riverbank and the distant shore. The world around them seemed to fade away, leaving only the dark waters of the river and the thick, swirling mist.

Elara could feel the river's magic pressing down on her, a heavy weight that seemed to seep into her very bones. The knot of anxiety in her chest tightened, her heart pounding with a mix of fear and anticipation. She knew that the river would show her something—something from her past, something she had tried to forget. But she also knew that she had to face it, had to confront whatever the river revealed, if she was to move forward.

Suddenly, the mist parted, revealing a narrow stone bridge that spanned the width of the river. The bridge was old and weathered, its surface slick with moisture, the stones cracked and crumbling with age. The mist swirled around the bridge like a shroud, the fog thick and impenetrable on either side.

"There," Lyra said, pointing to the bridge. "That's our way across."

Elara nodded, her gaze fixed on the bridge. "Be careful," she warned, her voice low and tense. "The river's magic is strong here. We have to stay focused, stay together."

With that, they stepped onto the bridge, the stones cold and slippery beneath their feet. The mist closed in around them, the world beyond the bridge fading into nothingness. The air was thick with tension, the silence oppressive, broken only by the soft sound of their footsteps on the stone.

As they reached the midpoint of the bridge, the mist seemed to grow thicker, swirling around them like a living thing. The air grew colder, the temperature dropping rapidly as the fog closed in, obscuring the riverbank and the distant shore.

And then, without warning, the world around them shifted.

Elara felt a sudden, dizzying sensation as the world seemed to tilt and spin, the bridge beneath her feet vanishing into the swirling mist. The air around her grew thick and heavy, pressing down on her like a physical weight. She tried to steady herself, to find her footing, but the world was spinning out of control, the mist closing in around her like a suffocating shroud.

And then, just as suddenly as it had begun, the spinning stopped. The mist cleared, revealing a new landscape—a place that was both familiar and strange, a place from her past.

Elara found herself standing in a small, sunlit clearing, the air filled with the scent of wildflowers and the sound of birdsong. The grass was soft and green beneath her feet, the sunlight warm on her skin. The clearing was surrounded by tall, ancient trees, their leaves rustling softly in the breeze.

But it was the figure standing in the center of the clearing that caught her attention—a woman with long, flowing hair and a gentle smile, her eyes filled with warmth and love.

"Mother?" Elara whispered, her heart pounding in her chest.

The woman turned to face her, her smile widening. "Elara, my dear," she said, her voice soft and soothing. "It's so good to see you."

Elara's breath caught in her throat, her eyes filling with tears. It had been so long since she had seen her mother, so long since that terrible day when she had lost her forever. And now, here she was, standing before her as if nothing had changed, as if the years of grief and loss had never happened.

"Mother, how... how are you here?" Elara asked, her voice trembling with emotion. "This can't be real."

Her mother smiled, her eyes filled with a deep, abiding love. "This is the River of Reflection, my dear," she said gently. "It shows you what is in your heart, what you long for most."

Elara's heart ached with longing as she stepped forward, reaching out to touch her mother's hand. The warmth of her mother's touch was real, solid, grounding her in this moment.

"I've missed you so much," Elara whispered, her voice breaking. "I've tried to be strong, tried to move on, but I've never stopped missing you."

Her mother's smile softened, and she reached out to cup Elara's cheek, her touch gentle and comforting. "I know, my dear," she said softly. "I've watched over you, seen the strength and courage you've shown. You've grown into a remarkable young woman, Elara. I'm so proud of you."

Elara felt a tear slip down her cheek, her heart swelling with a mix of love and sorrow. "But I failed you," she said, her voice filled with regret. "I couldn't save you. I wasn't strong enough."

Her mother's expression grew serious, her gaze filled with understanding. "Elara, you were just a child," she said gently. "There was nothing you could have done. My death was not your fault."

Elara shook her head, her tears flowing freely now. "But I should have done more. I should have—"

Her mother placed a finger to her lips, silencing her. "Elara, listen to me," she said, her voice firm but filled with love. "You did everything you could. You were brave and strong, and you've carried that strength with you all these years. But you must learn to forgive yourself, to let go of the guilt that has weighed you down for so long."

Elara's heart ached with the truth of her mother's words, the pain of her loss still raw and unhealed. But as she looked into her mother's eyes, she felt a warmth spreading through her, a sense of peace and acceptance that she had not felt in years.

"I've missed you so much," Elara whispered, her voice filled with emotion. "I wish you were still here."

Her mother smiled, her eyes shining with love. "I'm always with you, Elara," she said softly. "In your heart, in your memories. I will always be with you."

Elara closed her eyes, allowing herself to feel the warmth of her mother's love, the peace that came with knowing she was not alone. She knew that this moment, this vision, was a gift from the River of Reflection—a chance to confront her deepest regret, to find forgiveness and self-acceptance.

When she opened her eyes again, her mother was gone, the clearing around her fading into the swirling mist. Elara felt a sense of loss, but also a sense of peace, a weight lifted from her shoulders.

The mist cleared, revealing the stone bridge beneath her feet once more. She was back in the present, the River of Reflection flowing silently beneath her. Her companions stood nearby, each of them lost in their own thoughts, their faces reflecting the emotions of whatever visions the river had shown them.

Dain was the first to speak, his voice low and steady. "The river... it showed me my past," he said, his expression serious. "The mistakes I've made, the people

I've hurt. It's not easy to face those things, but I know now that I have to accept them, to learn from them."

Lyra nodded, her sharp eyes still clouded with the remnants of her vision. "The river showed me things I thought I'd buried, memories I didn't want to face. But I know now that I can't run from my past. I have to confront it, to make peace with it."

Breck grunted in agreement, his expression grim. "Aye, the river doesn't pull any punches. But it's a lesson we all need to learn."

Tomas looked pale and shaken, but there was a new determination in his eyes. "I saw my mentor," he said, his voice trembling slightly. "The one I couldn't save. But he told me... he told me that it wasn't my fault, that I did everything I could. I have to believe that."

Elara nodded, her heart swelling with pride and gratitude for her companions. They had all faced their deepest fears, their darkest regrets, and they had come through stronger for it.

"We've all been tested," she said, her voice filled with resolve. "But we've learned something important. We can't move forward if we're weighed down by the past. We have to accept it, learn from it, and then let it go."

Her companions nodded in agreement, their expressions resolute. The River of Reflection had shown them their pasts, their regrets, their fears, but it had also given them the chance to confront those things, to find peace and acceptance.

As they crossed the bridge and stepped onto the far shore, Elara felt a sense of renewal, a lightness in her heart that had not been there before. The journey ahead was still fraught with danger, the path uncertain, but she knew now that they were ready for whatever lay ahead.

They had faced the darkness of the forest, had confronted the sorcerer and lifted the curse, and now they had crossed the River of Reflection, each of them stronger and more determined than ever before.

The sun was rising higher in the sky now, its golden light casting long shadows across the landscape. The mist that had shrouded the river was beginning to lift, revealing the rolling hills and open plains beyond.

Elara took a deep breath, feeling the warmth of the sun on her face, the promise of a new day filling her with hope and determination.

"We're ready," she said softly, more to herself than to the others. "We're ready for whatever comes next."

Dain nodded, his expression serious but filled with a quiet confidence. "We are."

With that, they set off once more, their hearts lightened by the lessons they had learned at the River of Reflection. The path ahead was still uncertain, but they knew now that they had the strength to face it, together.

As they walked into the rising sun, Elara felt a sense of peace settle over her, a deep and abiding knowledge that they were on the right path, that they were closer than ever to finding the Mirror of Eldoria and fulfilling their destiny.

End of Chapter 6.

Chapter 7: The Guardian of the Bridge

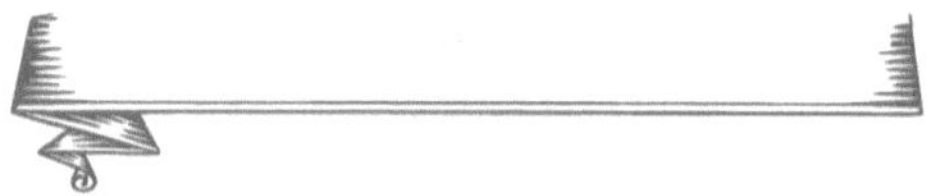

The journey along the River of Reflection had taken its toll on Elara and her companions. Though they had emerged from the trials of the river with a newfound sense of understanding and acceptance, the experience had left them emotionally drained. The memories they had confronted—the fears, regrets, and losses—still lingered in their minds like shadows, a reminder of the pain they had endured. But they had also gained something valuable: a deeper understanding of themselves and each other, and the knowledge that they could face whatever lay ahead with courage and resolve.

The sun was now high in the sky, its warm light casting a golden hue over the landscape. The mist that had clung to the riverbank was beginning to dissipate, revealing a wide, open plain that stretched out before them. The air was fresh and crisp, carrying the scent of wildflowers and the distant hum of insects. It was a stark contrast to the oppressive atmosphere of the river, and Elara felt a sense of relief as they stepped onto the far shore.

But their journey was far from over. The River of Reflection had been only the beginning of their trials, and Elara knew that the challenges ahead would only grow more difficult. The prophecy had spoken of many trials, of tests that would push them to their limits and force them to confront their deepest fears and desires. And as they continued their journey, the weight of that prophecy hung heavily over them, a constant reminder of the fate that awaited them.

As they walked along the riverbank, the landscape began to change once more. The rolling hills and open plains gave way to a rugged, rocky terrain, the ground uneven and treacherous underfoot. The air grew colder, the sky darkening as heavy clouds rolled in from the horizon. The once bright and open world was now shrouded in shadow, the light of the sun barely penetrating the thick, swirling clouds above.

It wasn't long before they saw it—a bridge that spanned the width of the river, its dark silhouette barely visible against the stormy sky. The bridge was old and weathered, its stone arches crumbling with age, but it was still intact, standing as a solitary sentinel over the rushing waters below. The river, which had been calm and reflective only a short time ago, was now a torrent, the water churning and frothing as it crashed against the rocky banks.

"There it is," Dain said, his voice low and tense as he pointed to the bridge. "The Bridge of Sacrifice."

Elara's heart skipped a beat at the name. The Bridge of Sacrifice was another place of legend, a place where travelers were tested not just in strength or courage, but in their willingness to give up something of great personal value. The guardian of the bridge, a fearsome creature of ancient magic, demanded a toll from those who sought to cross—a toll not of gold or treasure, but of sacrifice. It was said that the bridge had claimed many lives, that those who were unwilling or unable to make the sacrifice were cast into the river below, their bodies lost to the raging waters.

"We need to be prepared," Lyra said, her sharp eyes scanning the bridge for any signs of danger. "The guardian won't let us pass easily. We'll have to give up something valuable—something that means a great deal to us."

Breck, the blacksmith, grunted in agreement, his expression grim. "Aye, and it won't be easy. The bridge doesn't care about gold or riches. It wants something personal, something that's part of who we are."

Tomas, the healer's apprentice, looked pale and shaken, his eyes wide with fear. "But what if we don't have anything to give?" he asked, his voice trembling. "What if we can't make the sacrifice?"

Elara placed a reassuring hand on his shoulder, her voice gentle but firm. "We all have something to give, Tomas," she said. "It may not be easy, and it may be painful, but we have to be willing to make the sacrifice if we want to cross the bridge. This is part of our journey—part of the trials we must face."

Tomas nodded, though his fear was still palpable. "I'll try," he said, his voice barely above a whisper. "I'll do my best."

Elara smiled at him, though her own heart was heavy with the weight of the choice she knew she would soon have to make. The prophecy had spoken of sacrifice, of the need to give up something of great value in order to fulfill her destiny. She had always known that this moment would come, but now that it was here, the reality of it was almost too much to bear.

With a deep breath, she turned to her companions, her expression resolute. "We need to approach the bridge together," she said. "Whatever the guardian demands, we'll face it as a team. We've come this far together, and we'll get through this together."

Dain nodded, his expression serious. "Agreed. We'll face the guardian together, and we'll make the sacrifice together."

With a final nod of agreement, they approached the bridge, their steps slow and cautious. The wind had picked up, howling through the rocky terrain with a mournful wail that sent a shiver down Elara's spine. The air was thick with tension, the atmosphere heavy with a sense of impending doom.

As they reached the foot of the bridge, they saw it—the guardian, standing in the center of the bridge, its massive form blocking their path. The creature was unlike anything Elara had ever seen, a towering figure of ancient magic and raw power. Its body was covered in thick, black fur, its limbs muscular and powerful. It had the head of a wolf, with glowing red eyes that seemed to burn with an inner fire. Its teeth were long and sharp, bared in a snarl that sent a jolt of fear through Elara's heart.

But it wasn't just the creature's appearance that was terrifying—it was the aura of power that radiated from it, a dark and malevolent force that seemed to press down on them like a physical weight. The guardian was no ordinary beast—it was a creature of ancient magic, bound to the bridge by a powerful enchantment, its sole purpose to test those who sought to cross.

The guardian's eyes fixed on them as they approached, its gaze piercing and unyielding. It let out a low growl, a sound that rumbled through the air like thunder, shaking the very ground beneath their feet.

"Who dares to cross my bridge?" the guardian demanded, its voice deep and resonant, echoing off the stone walls of the bridge. "Who dares to challenge the toll?"

Elara took a deep breath, stepping forward to face the creature. "We are travelers," she said, her voice steady but filled with a sense of awe and fear. "We seek to cross the bridge and continue our journey."

The guardian's eyes narrowed, its growl deepening. "The bridge demands a toll," it said, its voice filled with dark power. "A toll not of gold or treasure, but of sacrifice. Each of you must give up something of great personal value—something that is a part of who you are. Only then will you be allowed to pass."

Elara felt her heart skip a beat at the guardian's words. She had known that the sacrifice would be difficult, but now that the moment was upon her, the reality of it was almost too much to bear. She had to give up something of great personal value—something that was a part of who she was.

But what could she give? What could she sacrifice that would satisfy the guardian's demands?

She glanced at her companions, seeing the same fear and uncertainty reflected in their eyes. They, too, were struggling with the choice they would have to make, the sacrifice they would have to offer.

Dain was the first to step forward, his expression grim but resolute. He reached into his pack and pulled out a small, worn leather pouch. Elara recognized it as the pouch Dain had carried with him since the beginning of their journey, the one he had never let out of his sight.

"This pouch contains the last remnants of my former life," Dain said, his voice steady but filled with emotion. "It holds the insignia of my knighthood, the one I swore to protect and serve. But that life is gone now, and I have chosen a new path. I offer this as my sacrifice."

The guardian's eyes gleamed with a dark light as it watched Dain place the pouch on the stone of the bridge. It let out a low growl of approval, nodding once in acknowledgment.

"Your sacrifice is accepted," the guardian said, its voice filled with a dark satisfaction. "You may pass."

Dain stepped back, his expression a mix of relief and sorrow. He had given up a piece of his past, a piece of who he was, but he had done so willingly, knowing that it was necessary for their journey to continue.

Lyra was next. She stepped forward, her sharp eyes narrowed in determination as she reached into her cloak and pulled out a small, ornate dagger. The dagger was intricately crafted, its hilt adorned with jewels and its blade razor-sharp. It was a weapon of great value, but it was also something more—it was a symbol of Lyra's past, of the life she had lived as a thief, a life she had left behind when she joined Elara's quest.

"This dagger was given to me by my sister," Lyra said, her voice steady but filled with a deep sadness. "It was the last gift she gave me before she betrayed me. I've carried it with me ever since, a reminder of the life I left behind. But now, I choose to let it go. I offer this as my sacrifice."

The guardian's eyes gleamed once more as it watched Lyra place the dagger on the stone of the bridge. It let out another growl of approval, nodding in acknowledgment.

"Your sacrifice is accepted," the guardian said, its voice filled with dark satisfaction. "You may pass."

Lyra stepped back, her expression a mix of relief and sorrow, much like Dain's. She had given up something of great personal value, something that had been a part of her for so long, but she had done so willingly, knowing that it was necessary for their journey to continue.

Breck was next. The burly blacksmith stepped forward, his expression grim as he reached into his pack and pulled out a small, worn hammer. The hammer was old and battered, its handle smooth from years of use, but it was clear that it held great sentimental value for Breck.

"This hammer belonged to my father," Breck said, his voice low and steady. "He taught me everything I know about smithing, about crafting weapons and tools. This hammer was his, and it was passed down to me when he died. It's a part of who I am, a part of my heritage. But I offer it now as my sacrifice."

The guardian watched with gleaming eyes as Breck placed the hammer on the stone of the bridge. It let out another growl of approval, nodding in acknowledgment.

"Your sacrifice is accepted," the guardian said, its voice filled with dark satisfaction. "You may pass."

Breck stepped back, his expression a mix of relief and sorrow. He had given up something that had been a part of him for so long, something that connected him to his past, but he had done so willingly, knowing that it was necessary for their journey to continue.

Tomas was last. The young healer's apprentice stepped forward, his hands trembling as he reached into his cloak and pulled out a small, leather-bound journal. The journal was old and worn, its pages filled with notes and sketches, a record of everything Tomas had learned during his apprenticeship.

"This journal belonged to my mentor," Tomas said, his voice trembling with emotion. "He gave it to me when I first began my training, and I've carried it with me ever since. It's a record of everything he taught me, everything I've learned. It's a part of who I am, a part of my journey as a healer. But I offer it now as my sacrifice."

The guardian's eyes gleamed with a dark light as it watched Tomas place the journal on the stone of the bridge. It let out another growl of approval, nodding in acknowledgment.

"Your sacrifice is accepted," the guardian said, its voice filled with dark satisfaction. "You may pass."

Tomas stepped back, his expression a mix of relief and sorrow. He had given up something that had been a part of him for so long, something that connected him to his mentor and his journey as a healer, but he had done so willingly, knowing that it was necessary for their journey to continue.

Finally, it was Elara's turn. She stepped forward, her heart pounding with fear and anticipation. She had watched as each of her companions had made their sacrifices, had given up something of great personal value, and now it was her turn. But what could she give? What could she sacrifice that would satisfy the guardian's demands?

She thought of the things she carried with her—the sword at her side, the cloak on her back, the small trinkets and mementos she had collected along the way. But none of them seemed right. None of them seemed valuable enough, personal enough, to satisfy the guardian's demands.

And then she remembered—her mother's locket.

The locket had been a gift from her mother, given to her on the day she had left Briar Glen to begin her journey. It was a small, simple locket, made of silver and engraved with a delicate floral pattern. Inside, it held a tiny portrait of her mother, a reminder of the love and warmth she had left behind.

Elara's heart ached at the thought of giving it up. The locket was more than just a piece of jewelry—it was a connection to her past, to the life she had lived before the prophecy had changed everything. It was a symbol of her mother's love, a reminder of the strength and courage that had carried her through the darkest moments of her journey.

But she knew that this was the sacrifice the guardian demanded. She had to give up something of great personal value, something that was a part of who she was. And the locket was the most precious thing she had, the thing that meant the most to her.

With trembling hands, she reached into her cloak and pulled out the locket, holding it in her palm as she stepped forward. The guardian's eyes fixed on the locket, its gaze piercing and unyielding.

"This locket belonged to my mother," Elara said, her voice trembling with emotion. "It was a gift from her, a reminder of the love and strength she gave me. It's a part of who I am, a part of my past. But I offer it now as my sacrifice."

The guardian's eyes gleamed with a dark light as it watched Elara place the locket on the stone of the bridge. It let out a final growl of approval, nodding in acknowledgment.

"Your sacrifice is accepted," the guardian said, its voice filled with dark satisfaction. "You may pass."

Elara stepped back, her heart heavy with the weight of the sacrifice she had just made. She had given up the most precious thing she had, the locket that had connected her to her mother and her past. But she had done so willingly, knowing that it was necessary for their journey to continue.

As they crossed the bridge, the air around them seemed to lighten, the oppressive weight of the guardian's presence lifting as they left the toll behind. The dark, swirling clouds above began to part, allowing the golden light of the sun to shine through once more.

The other side of the bridge was a stark contrast to the rugged, rocky terrain they had just left behind. The ground was soft and green, covered in a carpet of wildflowers that swayed gently in the breeze. The air was filled with the scent of blooming flowers and the distant hum of insects, a reminder of the beauty and life that still existed in the world.

But despite the beauty of the landscape, Elara couldn't shake the sense of loss that hung over her. The locket had been more than just a piece of jewelry—it had been a symbol of her mother's love, a connection to the life she had left behind. And now it was gone, sacrificed to the guardian of the bridge.

Her companions, too, seemed to feel the weight of their sacrifices. Dain's expression was grim, his hand resting on the empty space at his side where the pouch had once hung. Lyra's eyes were clouded with a deep sadness, her hand brushing the empty space at her belt where the dagger had once been. Breck's gaze was distant, his hand resting on the empty space at his side where the hammer had once been. And Tomas's expression was one of quiet sorrow, his hand resting on the empty space at his side where the journal had once been.

But despite the sense of loss, there was also a sense of relief—a sense that they had passed the test, had made the necessary sacrifices to continue their journey. They had faced the guardian of the bridge, had given up something of great personal value, and had been allowed to pass.

As they walked through the field of wildflowers, the golden light of the sun casting long shadows across the landscape, Elara felt a sense of peace begin to settle over her. The journey ahead was still uncertain, the challenges still daunting, but they had proven that they were willing to make the sacrifices necessary to fulfill their destiny.

They had faced the darkness of the forest, had confronted the sorcerer and lifted the curse, had crossed the River of Reflection and the Bridge of Sacrifice, and they were closer than ever to finding the Mirror of Eldoria.

As the sun began to set, casting a warm, golden light over the landscape, Elara felt a sense of hope and determination fill her heart. The journey ahead would be long and difficult, but she knew that they were ready for whatever lay ahead.

Together, they would find the mirror, fulfill the prophecy, and lift the curse that had plagued the land for so long. They would overcome the trials and challenges that awaited them, and they would do it as a team—united by the sacrifices they had made, and the bonds they had forged along the way.

And as they walked into the fading light, the stars beginning to twinkle in the darkening sky, Elara knew that they were on the right path—closer than ever to fulfilling their destiny and bringing peace to the kingdom.

END OF CHAPTER 7.

Chapter 8: The Desert of Lost Time

The land stretched out before them in a vast, seemingly endless expanse of golden sand, the horizon shimmering in the heat. The sun blazed high in the sky, casting sharp, unforgiving shadows across the desert landscape. The air was dry and oppressive, the heat radiating off the ground in waves that distorted the view ahead. It was as if they had stepped into another world—a world where time itself seemed to blur and shift, its boundaries uncertain and elusive.

Elara and her companions stood at the edge of the Desert of Lost Time, their expressions a mix of awe and trepidation. The tales they had heard of this place spoke of its strange and unpredictable nature, where time did not flow in a linear fashion but instead twisted and turned upon itself, making it nearly impossible to navigate. It was said that travelers who entered the desert could find themselves trapped for years, or emerge on the other side having lost only a few minutes, the passage of time a mystery beyond comprehension.

"This is it," Dain said, his voice low and tense as he gazed out at the desert. "The Desert of Lost Time."

Elara nodded, her heart pounding in her chest. The desert was the next trial in their journey, a place of great danger but also great significance. The prophecy had mentioned the desert, describing it as a place where the flow of time was controlled by an ancient, hidden power—a power that they would need to uncover if they were to escape its grasp.

"We have to be careful," Lyra said, her sharp eyes scanning the horizon for any signs of movement. "Time doesn't work the same way here. We could get lost, or worse."

Breck grunted in agreement, his expression grim. "Aye, and we'll need to find shelter quickly. The sun's unforgiving out here, and the nights are just as deadly."

Tomas, the healer's apprentice, looked pale and nervous, his eyes wide with fear. "How are we supposed to navigate this place?" he asked, his voice trembling. "If time doesn't work the way it should, how will we know how long we've been here, or how far we've traveled?"

Elara placed a reassuring hand on his shoulder, her voice calm but firm. "We'll have to rely on each other," she said. "We'll keep moving, stay focused, and trust that we can find the way through. We've faced challenges before, and we've come through stronger for it. This is just another trial, another test of our resolve."

Tomas nodded, though his fear was still evident. "I'll do my best," he said, his voice barely above a whisper.

With a final nod to her companions, Elara led the way into the desert, her heart heavy with the weight of the task ahead. The sand shifted beneath their feet as they walked, the grains hot and unforgiving, each step an effort against the harsh environment. The sun beat down on them mercilessly, its heat oppressive and stifling, and the air was thick with the scent of dry earth and dust.

The desert was eerily silent, the only sound the soft crunch of their footsteps on the sand. There were no signs of life, no plants or animals to break the monotony of the endless dunes. The landscape was barren and featureless, the horizon a distant, shimmering line that seemed to recede further with every step they took.

As they walked, Elara couldn't shake the feeling that something was wrong. Time felt strange here—slippery and elusive, as if it were constantly shifting and changing around them. One moment, the sun was high in the sky, the heat unbearable, and the next, it seemed to dip toward the horizon, casting long shadows across the sand. The passage of time was impossible to track, and Elara felt a growing sense of unease as they ventured deeper into the desert.

"How long have we been walking?" Lyra asked, her voice tense as she glanced at the sun, which now hung low in the sky, casting the landscape in a golden glow.

Elara frowned, trying to recall how long it had been since they entered the desert, but her memory was hazy, as if the details were slipping away from her grasp. "I'm not sure," she admitted, her voice filled with uncertainty. "It feels like hours, but it could have been only minutes... or days."

Dain shook his head, his expression grim. "This place is playing tricks on us. We need to stay focused, keep moving forward. If we stop now, we might lose track of time completely."

Breck nodded in agreement, his gaze fixed on the horizon. "Aye, we need to find shelter soon. The sun's setting, and the temperature's going to drop quickly. We can't afford to be caught out here when night falls."

Elara knew he was right. The desert nights were just as deadly as the days, the temperature dropping to freezing levels as soon as the sun disappeared. They needed to find shelter, and quickly, before the cold set in.

As they continued their journey, the landscape began to change once more. The sand dunes grew taller, their edges sharp and defined against the darkening sky. The air grew colder, the heat of the day dissipating rapidly as the sun dipped below the horizon, casting the desert in a deep, velvety twilight.

It was then that they saw it—a faint, flickering light in the distance, barely visible against the darkness of the desert. The light was small and dim, but it was a sign of life, a beacon of hope in the vast, empty wasteland.

"There!" Dain exclaimed, pointing toward the light. "There's someone out there! Maybe they can help us!"

Elara felt a surge of hope as she turned toward the light, her heart racing with anticipation. If there were people out there, then there was a chance they could find shelter, a chance they could survive the night.

With renewed determination, they made their way toward the light, their pace quickening as the cold began to seep into their bones. The air was frigid now, the temperature dropping rapidly with the setting sun, and the sand beneath their feet grew colder and harder with each step.

As they approached the light, they saw that it came from a small, makeshift camp nestled at the base of a towering sand dune. The camp was simple—a few tattered tents, a small fire pit, and several figures huddled around the fire, their faces hidden in the shadows.

Elara felt a sense of unease as they drew closer. The figures around the fire were still and silent, their heads bowed as if in prayer or deep contemplation. There was something strange about the scene, something unsettling that she couldn't quite place.

But they had no choice. They needed shelter, and these people were their only hope.

"Hello?" Elara called out as they approached the camp, her voice echoing in the stillness of the desert. "We're travelers, and we need shelter for the night. Can you help us?"

The figures around the fire did not respond, did not even lift their heads to acknowledge her presence. They remained still and silent, their faces hidden in the flickering shadows.

Elara felt a shiver run down her spine, her sense of unease growing stronger. There was something wrong here, something unnatural.

But before she could turn away, one of the figures slowly raised its head, its eyes locking onto hers with an intensity that took her breath away.

The figure was an old woman, her face lined with deep wrinkles, her eyes dark and hollow. She was dressed in tattered robes, her hair a wild tangle of gray and white. There was something ancient and otherworldly about her, something that made Elara feel as if she were staring into the eyes of someone who had seen centuries pass in the blink of an eye.

"Travelers," the old woman said, her voice low and raspy, as if it had not been used in a long time. "You have come to the Desert of Lost Time."

Elara nodded, her throat dry and tight. "Yes," she said, her voice barely above a whisper. "We're trying to cross the desert, but we've lost our way. Can you help us?"

The old woman's gaze never wavered, her dark eyes boring into Elara's soul. "You seek to escape the desert," she said, her voice filled with a deep, sorrowful wisdom. "But time does not flow as it should here. The desert is a place of lost moments, of forgotten years. Those who enter may never leave."

Elara felt a chill run down her spine, her heart pounding in her chest. "But there must be a way," she said, her voice trembling with desperation. "There must be a way to escape."

The old woman was silent for a long moment, her gaze never leaving Elara's. Then, slowly, she nodded. "There is a way," she said, her voice filled with a deep sadness. "But it is not an easy path. The desert is controlled by an ancient timepiece, hidden deep within its sands. It is the source of the desert's power, the key to controlling the flow of time. If you can find it, you may be able to escape."

Elara's heart skipped a beat at the old woman's words. A timepiece—a device that controlled the flow of time. It was the answer they had been searching for, the key to escaping the desert and continuing their journey.

"Where is this timepiece?" Elara asked, her voice filled with determination. "How do we find it?"

The old woman's gaze darkened, her expression filled with sorrow. "The timepiece is hidden in the heart of the desert, guarded by the spirits of those who have been

lost to time. It is a dangerous journey, one that few have survived. But if you are determined, if you are willing to face the trials ahead, you may find it."

Elara nodded, her resolve firm. "We have no choice," she said. "We must find the timepiece and escape this desert."

The old woman studied her for a long moment, her eyes filled with a deep, ancient wisdom. Then she nodded slowly, as if coming to a decision.

"Very well," she said, her voice low and steady. "I will help you. But you must be prepared for the challenges ahead. The desert will test you, will push you to your limits. But if you stay true to your path, you may find the timepiece and escape this place."

With that, the old woman turned and began to gather her belongings, her movements slow and deliberate. The other figures around the fire remained silent and still, their faces hidden in the shadows.

Elara felt a sense of unease as she watched the old woman prepare for their journey. There was something strange about this place, something unsettling that she couldn't quite place. But they had no choice. They needed to find the timepiece, and this woman was their only hope.

The old woman led them deeper into the desert, her steps sure and steady as she navigated the shifting sands. The air was cold now, the temperature dropping rapidly as the night set in. The stars above were sharp and bright, their light casting a pale glow over the landscape.

They walked in silence, the only sound the soft crunch of their footsteps on the sand. The desert was vast and empty, the horizon stretching out in all directions, a never-ending sea of sand and sky. The sense of time slipping away, of moments lost and forgotten, was stronger than ever, a constant reminder of the danger they faced.

As they traveled, the old woman began to speak, her voice low and steady. "The desert is a place of lost time," she said. "It is a place where moments slip away, where years can be lost in the blink of an eye. Those who enter often find themselves trapped, their lives slipping away as time stretches and contracts around them."

Elara listened intently, her heart heavy with the weight of the old woman's words. The desert was more than just a physical place—it was a place of magic, a place where time itself was fluid and unpredictable. And they were at its mercy, their fate uncertain.

"But the timepiece," Elara said, her voice filled with determination. "It can control the flow of time, can't it? If we find it, we can escape."

The old woman nodded, her expression serious. "Yes, the timepiece controls the flow of time in the desert. It is an ancient artifact, created long ago by a powerful sorcerer. But it is also a dangerous device, one that can be easily misused. Many have sought it, but few have survived the journey to find it."

Elara felt a chill run down her spine at the old woman's words. The timepiece was their only hope of escaping the desert, but it was also a powerful and dangerous artifact. They would need to be careful, to use it wisely if they were to survive.

The night deepened as they traveled, the cold biting at their skin as the temperature continued to drop. The stars above were sharp and bright, their light casting a pale glow over the landscape. The sense of time slipping away, of moments lost and forgotten, was stronger than ever, a constant reminder of the danger they faced.

After what felt like hours of walking, they finally reached their destination—a massive sand dune that towered over the desert, its peak lost in the darkness of the night. The old woman stopped at the base of the dune, her gaze fixed on the ground beneath her feet.

"This is the place," she said, her voice low and steady. "The timepiece is buried here, deep within the sands. But be warned—the spirits of those who have been lost to time guard it fiercely. They will not let you take it without a fight."

Elara's heart pounded in her chest as she gazed up at the towering dune. The timepiece was buried here, the key to their escape, but it was also guarded by the spirits of the lost—spirits that would stop at nothing to protect it.

But they had no choice. They needed to find the timepiece, and they needed to do it quickly. The longer they stayed in the desert, the greater the risk of losing themselves to its strange and unpredictable nature.

With a deep breath, Elara nodded. "We're ready," she said, her voice filled with determination. "We'll find the timepiece and escape this desert."

The old woman nodded, her expression serious. "Very well," she said. "But be careful. The spirits are powerful, and they will do everything in their power to stop you."

With that, she stepped back, allowing Elara and her companions to take the lead. They began to climb the dune, the sand shifting beneath their feet as they made their way to the top. The air was cold and still, the only sound the soft crunch of their footsteps on the sand.

As they climbed, the sense of time slipping away, of moments lost and forgotten, grew stronger. The desert seemed to stretch out before them, a never-ending sea of sand and sky, the horizon receding further with every step they took. The stars above were sharp and bright, their light casting a pale glow over the landscape.

When they finally reached the top of the dune, Elara felt a surge of hope as she saw the timepiece—a small, ornate hourglass, half-buried in the sand at the center of the dune. The hourglass was made of gold, its surface etched with intricate patterns and symbols, the sand inside glowing with a soft, otherworldly light.

But as she reached out to take it, the air around them suddenly grew cold, and a low, mournful wail filled the night. The sand beneath their feet began to shift and churn, rising up in swirling clouds as ghostly figures emerged from the dunes—spirits of those who had been lost to time, their forms twisted and distorted by the desert's magic.

The spirits moved toward them with an eerie, unnatural grace, their eyes glowing with a cold, malevolent light. They circled around the timepiece, their voices rising in a haunting, discordant chorus that sent shivers down Elara's spine.

"We must protect the timepiece," one of the spirits intoned, its voice low and hollow. "It is our duty. It is our curse."

Elara felt a surge of fear as the spirits closed in around them, their forms flickering and shifting in the dim light of the stars. But she knew they couldn't back down now. The timepiece was their only hope of escaping the desert, and they had to take it, no matter the cost.

With a deep breath, she drew her sword, the blade gleaming in the pale light of the stars. "We're not here to harm you," she said, her voice steady but filled with determination. "We just need the timepiece. We need to escape this desert."

The spirits let out another mournful wail, their voices rising in a discordant chorus that echoed through the night. "You cannot take it," one of the spirits said, its voice filled with a deep, haunting sorrow. "We are bound to protect it. We cannot let you pass."

Elara tightened her grip on her sword, her heart pounding in her chest. "I'm sorry," she said, her voice filled with regret. "But we have no choice."

With that, she lunged forward, her sword cutting through the air as she aimed for the nearest spirit. The blade passed through the ghostly figure with no resistance, the spirit dissolving into a cloud of mist that was quickly swept away by the wind.

But more spirits rose up from the sand to take its place, their forms swirling and shifting as they closed in around them. Elara felt a surge of desperation as she fought to keep them at bay, her sword cutting through the air in a desperate attempt to protect the timepiece.

Her companions joined the fight, their weapons flashing in the dim light as they battled the spirits. Dain's sword cut through the ghostly figures with a deadly precision, while Lyra's daggers flashed in the darkness, striking down any spirit that came too close. Breck swung his hammer with a fierce determination, the weapon glowing with a faint, otherworldly light as it connected with the spirits, sending them back into the sand from which they had emerged.

But the spirits were relentless, their numbers seemingly endless as they rose up from the dunes to protect the timepiece. Elara felt her strength beginning to wane, her movements growing slower and more sluggish as the battle wore on. The desert's magic was taking its toll, the sense of time slipping away growing stronger with each passing moment.

And then, just as she thought she couldn't fight any longer, she heard a voice—a soft, melodic voice that seemed to cut through the chaos of the battle, filling her with a sense of calm and clarity.

"Elara," the voice said, its tone gentle and soothing. "You must take the timepiece. It is the only way to escape."

Elara turned toward the source of the voice, her heart pounding with a mix of fear and hope. Standing at the edge of the dune was the old woman, her dark eyes filled with a deep, ancient wisdom.

"But the spirits—" Elara began, her voice trembling with fear.

The old woman shook her head, her gaze steady. "The spirits are bound to protect the timepiece," she said. "But they are also bound by time. If you take the timepiece, you can control the flow of time

in the desert. You can stop them."

Elara felt a surge of determination at the old woman's words. The timepiece was the key to escaping the desert, to controlling the flow of time and stopping the spirits. But she would have to be quick—she would have to take it before the spirits could stop her.

With a deep breath, she lunged forward, her hand reaching out to grasp the hourglass. The spirits let out a mournful wail as she touched the timepiece, their forms flickering and shifting as the flow of time in the desert began to change.

The sand inside the hourglass began to glow with a bright, golden light, the grains moving rapidly as time began to shift and flow around them. The spirits let out one final, mournful wail before dissolving into the sand, their forms swept away by the wind.

Elara felt a surge of relief as the spirits disappeared, the air around them growing still and quiet. The timepiece was warm in her hand, the glow of the sand inside casting a soft, golden light over the desert.

With the timepiece in her possession, the flow of time in the desert was under her control. She could feel its power, its ancient magic pulsing through her, connecting her to the very fabric of time itself.

"Elara, you did it," Dain said, his voice filled with awe as he approached her. "You've stopped the spirits."

Elara nodded, her heart still racing from the battle. "We have the timepiece," she said, her voice filled with a mix of relief and determination. "We can escape the desert."

The old woman stepped forward, her gaze fixed on the hourglass in Elara's hand. "The timepiece is a powerful artifact," she said, her voice low and steady.

"But it is also dangerous. You must use it wisely, Elara. It can control the flow of time, but it can also consume you if you're not careful."

Elara nodded, her grip on the timepiece tightening. She could feel its power, its ancient magic pulsing through her, and she knew that the old woman's words were true. The timepiece was their only hope of escaping the desert, but it was also a dangerous and unpredictable artifact.

"We'll be careful," she said, her voice filled with resolve. "But we have to use it to escape. We can't stay here any longer."

The old woman nodded, her gaze filled with a deep, ancient wisdom. "Very well," she said. "But remember, Elara—time is a powerful force. It is not something to be taken lightly."

With that, the old woman turned and began to walk away, her steps slow and deliberate as she disappeared into the darkness of the desert.

Elara watched her go, her heart heavy with the weight of the responsibility she now carried. The timepiece was their only hope of escaping the desert, but it was also a powerful and dangerous artifact. They would need to use it wisely, to control the flow of time in the desert and find their way out.

As they began their journey back to the edge of the desert, Elara felt a sense of hope and determination fill her heart. The journey ahead would be long and difficult, but they had the timepiece—they had the key to controlling the flow of time and escaping the desert.

With each step, the landscape around them began to shift and change, the flow of time in the desert now under their control. The sun rose and set in the sky in a matter of moments, the passage of days and nights blurring together as they made their way through the shifting sands.

Finally, after what felt like hours of walking, they reached the edge of the desert, the vast expanse of sand giving way to a lush, green landscape that stretched out before them. The air was warm and fragrant, filled with the scent of blooming flowers and the distant hum of insects.

Elara felt a surge of relief as they stepped out of the desert, the sense of time slipping away finally fading as they left the sands behind. The timepiece was still warm in her hand, its golden light casting a soft glow over the landscape.

"We made it," Dain said, his voice filled with awe as he gazed out at the green landscape before them. "We escaped the desert."

Elara nodded, her heart swelling with a mix of relief and determination. "We did," she said, her voice filled with resolve. "But our journey isn't over yet. We still have to find the Mirror of Eldoria."

Her companions nodded in agreement, their expressions filled with a renewed sense of purpose. They had escaped the Desert of Lost Time, had faced the trials and challenges of the sands, and they were stronger for it.

As they walked into the lush, green landscape, the timepiece glowing softly in Elara's hand, she felt a deep sense of hope and determination fill her heart. The journey ahead would be long and difficult, but they had proven that they were capable of overcoming any challenge, of facing any trial.

Together, they would find the Mirror of Eldoria, fulfill the prophecy, and bring peace to the kingdom. They would face whatever challenges lay ahead, and they would do it as a team—united by the sacrifices they had made, and the bonds they had forged along the way.

And as they walked into the bright, golden light of the new day, the future stretched out before them, filled with hope and promise.

End of Chapter 8.

Chapter 9: The Enchanted Oasis

The exhaustion of the desert hung over Elara and her companions like a heavy cloak. They had crossed the Desert of Lost Time, a place where the sun and moon danced unpredictably across the sky, where days stretched into eternity or slipped away in a heartbeat. The timepiece that Elara now carried in her pack had been their salvation, but the journey had left them all weary in body and spirit. As they emerged from the endless sands and entered a new landscape, the change was so sudden and stark that it felt almost like a dream.

Ahead of them lay a lush oasis, a paradise of greenery and sparkling water nestled among towering palm trees. The air, which had been dry and searing in the desert, was now cool and fragrant, filled with the scent of blooming flowers and the distant sound of flowing water. The sun, which had blazed mercilessly overhead for what felt like days, was now gentle and warm, casting dappled light through the canopy of leaves.

Elara stopped at the edge of the oasis, her breath catching in her throat. After the harsh, unrelenting desert, this place seemed like a miracle, a gift from the gods to reward their perseverance.

"Look," Lyra said, her voice filled with wonder as she pointed to the crystal-clear pool of water that lay at the heart of the oasis. "Water—fresh, clean water. We've made it."

Breck let out a sigh of relief, his shoulders slumping as he gazed at the oasis. "Finally," he said, his voice heavy with exhaustion. "A place to rest, to recover. We deserve this."

Tomas, the healer's apprentice, could hardly contain his excitement as he took in the sight of the vibrant flowers, the soft green grass, and the clear water. "It's beautiful," he said, his voice trembling with emotion. "After everything we've been through, this is exactly what we needed."

Even Dain, who was usually cautious and wary, allowed himself a small smile as he surveyed the oasis. "It seems we've found a bit of luck at last," he said, his voice filled with quiet satisfaction.

Elara, however, couldn't shake a nagging feeling of unease that had settled in the pit of her stomach. The oasis was indeed beautiful, but it was also unexpected. The transition from the desolate, harsh desert to this lush paradise was so sudden, so abrupt, that it felt almost unnatural. And then there was the prophecy, the warnings from the old sage about the trials they would face on their journey to find the Mirror of Eldoria. Nothing on this quest had come easily, and she doubted that this oasis would be any different.

Still, the temptation to rest, to drink from the cool waters and lie in the shade of the trees, was strong. Her body ached from the long journey, her muscles sore and tired. The promise of relief, even if only for a short time, was almost irresistible.

"We should be cautious," Elara said, her voice laced with the caution she felt. "This place seems too perfect, too convenient. It could be a trap."

Dain looked at her, his brow furrowed in concern. "A trap? What kind of trap?"

Elara shook her head, her gaze sweeping over the oasis. "I don't know, but we can't let our guard down. We've been through too much to lose our focus now."

Lyra, who had already taken a few steps toward the water, paused and turned back to Elara, her expression one of both understanding and frustration. "Elara, we've been walking for days without proper rest. The desert was unforgiving, and we barely made it through. We need to recover our strength, or we won't stand a chance in the trials ahead."

Breck nodded in agreement, his tired eyes reflecting the same sentiment. "Aye, lass. We can't keep going like this without a break. We need to rest, to heal. This oasis might be just what we need."

Tomas looked from one companion to the next, uncertainty clouding his face. "But what if Elara's right? What if there's something wrong with this place?"

Elara sighed, feeling the weight of their exhaustion pressing down on her. She knew they were right—they did need to rest, to recover from the ordeal of the desert. But she couldn't shake the feeling that something was amiss, that this oasis was not what it seemed.

"We'll rest," she said finally, her voice tinged with reluctance. "But we'll stay vigilant. We can't let our guard down completely."

Dain nodded in agreement, his expression serious. "We'll take turns keeping watch. We've come too far to be caught off guard now."

With that, the group made their way into the oasis, their steps slow and deliberate as they approached the pool of water. The air grew cooler as they entered the shade of the palm trees, the sound of the flowing water growing louder and more soothing.

They gathered around the edge of the pool, gazing into the clear, cool water. The surface was smooth and still, reflecting the sky and the surrounding trees like a mirror. Elara knelt beside the pool, dipping her hand into the water. It was refreshingly cool to the touch, and she felt a wave of relief wash over her as she scooped up a handful of water and brought it to her lips.

The water was pure and clean, its taste crisp and refreshing. She drank deeply, feeling the cool liquid soothe her parched throat and revive her tired body. The others followed suit, drinking from the pool with a sense of reverence and gratitude.

After they had drunk their fill, they settled down on the soft grass beneath the trees, the gentle breeze rustling the leaves above. The air was filled with the scent of blooming flowers, and the sound of the water was like a lullaby, soothing and calming.

Elara leaned back against the trunk of a tree, her eyes half-closed as she allowed herself to relax for the first time in what felt like days. The tension in her muscles began to ease, and she felt the weight of exhaustion lift from her shoulders.

But even as she allowed herself to rest, a part of her remained alert, her mind turning over the possibilities, the potential dangers that might lurk beneath the surface of this seemingly perfect oasis.

Time passed in a blur, the sun shifting slowly across the sky as the hours slipped away. The warmth of the sun, the coolness of the shade, and the gentle sound of the water combined to create a sense of peace and tranquility that was almost hypnotic.

As the sun began to dip toward the horizon, casting long shadows across the oasis, Elara's eyes fluttered open. She felt disoriented, as if she had just woken from a deep sleep, though she couldn't remember falling asleep in the first place.

She glanced around, her gaze falling on her companions, who were all still resting beneath the trees. Dain was lying on his back, his eyes closed as he breathed deeply, a look of contentment on his face. Lyra was sitting with her back against a tree, her eyes closed and a faint smile playing on her lips. Breck was stretched out on the grass, his arms crossed over his chest, while Tomas was lying on his side, his breathing slow and steady.

Elara frowned, a sense of unease creeping back into her mind. They had all been so tired, so desperate for rest, that they had allowed themselves to be lulled into a false sense of security. The oasis was too perfect, too convenient—and now, they had all let their guard down.

She pushed herself to her feet, her movements slow and deliberate as she tried to shake off the lingering sense of disorientation. The air felt heavier now, the warmth of the sun oppressive rather than soothing. The gentle breeze that had rustled the leaves earlier had stilled, and the sound of the water, once so soothing, now seemed to carry an underlying note of menace.

"Elara?" Tomas's voice broke the silence, and Elara turned to see the healer's apprentice sitting up, his expression dazed and confused. "What's happening? How long have we been here?"

Elara shook her head, her brow furrowing in concern. "I don't know. I... I can't remember."

Tomas's eyes widened in alarm as he looked around the oasis. "Something's not right," he said, his voice trembling. "We need to get out of here."

Elara nodded, her heart pounding in her chest. She had felt it too—that sense of something being wrong, of time slipping away from them. They had been so eager to rest, to recover from the hardships of the desert, that they had let their guard down, and now they were trapped in an enchantment, one that was luring them into forgetting their quest.

She moved quickly to rouse the others, shaking Dain's shoulder and calling out to Lyra and Breck. But they were slow to respond, their movements sluggish and their expressions confused.

"What's going on?" Dain asked groggily as he sat up, rubbing his eyes. "Did we sleep through the night?"

"I don't know," Elara replied, her voice urgent. "But we need to get moving. This place—it's not what it seems. We're being enchanted, lulled into forgetting why we're here."

Lyra blinked, her eyes narrowing as she tried to focus. "Enchanted? What do you mean?"

Elara's mind raced as she tried to find the words to explain the growing sense of danger she felt. "This oasis—it's too perfect, too convenient. We've been here for hours, but it feels like no time has passed at all. We're losing track of time, of our purpose. If we stay here any longer, we'll forget why we came here in the first place."

Breck frowned, his brow furrowing in confusion. "But why would anyone want to enchant us? We're just travelers."

Elara shook her head, her heart pounding with a sense of urgency. "I don't know, but we can't stay here. We need to leave—now."

But even as she said the words, she felt a strange reluctance to move, a heaviness in her limbs that made it difficult to take action. The enchantment was powerful, designed to lull them into a false sense of security, to make them forget their quest and lose themselves in the peaceful beauty of the oasis.

It was then that a voice from the past echoed in her mind, a voice filled with wisdom and a deep understanding of the trials they would face. It was the voice of the old sage who had first told her of the prophecy, the man who had set her on this path.

"Beware the temptations along your journey, Elara," the old sage had said, his voice filled with a quiet intensity. "Not all dangers come in the form of monsters or traps. Some will seek to deceive you, to lull you into forgetting your purpose. You must remain vigilant, for the path to the Mirror of Eldoria is fraught with such temptations."

Elara's eyes widened as the memory of the sage's words brought clarity to her mind. This was the temptation he had warned her about—a place designed to make them forget, to distract them from their quest. The oasis was an illusion, a trap set to ensnare them and keep them from fulfilling their destiny.

"We have to go," Elara said, her voice filled with newfound resolve. "This place—it's an illusion. We're being enchanted, and if we don't leave now, we'll never remember why we're here."

Her companions, still groggy and confused, looked at her with varying degrees of understanding and concern. But Elara could see that the enchantment was strong, its pull almost impossible to resist.

"We need to focus," Elara said urgently, her voice cutting through the haze that clouded their minds. "Remember the prophecy, remember why we're here. We have to find the Mirror of Eldoria—we can't let this place distract us."

Dain's eyes sharpened as he seemed to shake off the lingering effects of the enchantment. "You're right," he said, his voice steady. "We've been lulled into a false sense of security. We can't let our guard down now."

Lyra nodded slowly, her expression serious as she rose to her feet. "This oasis—it's too perfect. We should have known something was wrong."

Breck grunted in agreement, his expression grim. "Aye, we let ourselves get too comfortable. We need to get moving."

Tomas, though still visibly shaken, nodded as well. "Let's go," he said, his voice filled with determination. "We can't stay here."

With their minds now clear and their purpose restored, the group gathered their belongings and prepared to leave the oasis. The enchantment was still present, its pull strong and insistent, but Elara's determination—and the memory of the prophecy—gave them the strength to resist.

As they made their way back to the edge of the oasis, the landscape around them seemed to shift and change, the vibrant colors fading to reveal the true nature of the place. The grass beneath their feet withered and turned to dust, the water in the pool grew murky and stagnant, and the trees that had once provided shade were now twisted and gnarled, their branches bare and lifeless.

The illusion was breaking, the enchantment unraveling as they pushed forward, their resolve stronger than the magic that sought to trap them.

But as they reached the edge of the oasis, a figure appeared before them—a tall, slender woman with flowing hair and eyes that shimmered with a mesmerizing light. She was beautiful, her presence both alluring and intimidating, and her voice was like the sweetest music as she spoke.

"Why do you seek to leave, travelers?" the woman asked, her voice filled with a strange, compelling warmth. "You have found peace here, rest and comfort. There is no need to continue your journey. Stay with me, and I will give you everything you desire."

Elara felt the pull of the woman's words, a deep yearning to stay, to give in to the promise of comfort and safety. But she knew it was a lie, a trap designed to keep them from their quest.

"We can't stay," Elara said, her voice firm despite the temptation that tugged at her heart. "We have a purpose, a destiny to fulfill. We can't let ourselves be distracted."

The woman's eyes darkened, her smile fading as she stepped closer, her voice taking on a sharper, more insistent tone. "Why continue on a path of hardship and pain? Here, you can be safe, happy. The world beyond is filled with dangers—why face them when you can stay here, in peace?"

Dain stepped forward, his expression resolute. "We've come too far to turn back now. We can't be swayed by false promises."

The woman's gaze shifted to him, her eyes narrowing. "And what if you fail? What if the journey ahead destroys you? Here, you will have everything you need—no pain, no fear, only peace."

But Breck shook his head, his voice gruff and unwavering. "There's no peace in forgetting who we are, in abandoning our quest. We've faced worse than this, and we'll face whatever comes next."

Lyra nodded, her eyes sharp as she met the woman's gaze. "We won't be trapped by illusions. We know who we are, and we know what we need to do."

Tomas, though still visibly shaken, added his voice to theirs. "We can't stay here. We have to keep going."

The woman's eyes blazed with anger as she realized that her enchantment had failed, that her promises had been rejected. Her beautiful face twisted with fury, and the air around her seemed to shimmer with dark, malevolent energy.

"Fools!" she hissed, her voice no longer sweet and melodic but sharp and cutting. "You dare defy me? You dare reject my gifts?"

Elara stood her ground, her heart pounding with a mix of fear and determination. "We know what we must do," she said, her voice steady and clear. "We won't be swayed by illusions."

The woman's eyes narrowed, her voice filled with venom as she spoke. "Then you shall face the consequences of your choice. The path ahead will be fraught with dangers beyond your imagining. You will suffer, you will despair—but do not say that I did not offer you peace."

With those words, the woman vanished, her form dissolving into a cloud of mist that was quickly swept away by the wind. The enchantment that had held the oasis together crumbled, the last remnants of its illusion fading into nothingness.

The group stood in silence for a moment, the weight of what they had just faced settling over them like a heavy shroud. They had resisted the temptation, had broken free from the enchantment, but the journey ahead was still uncertain, the challenges still daunting.

Elara took a deep breath, her resolve stronger than ever. They had overcome the enchantment, had resisted the false promises of the oasis, and they were ready to face whatever came next.

"We did it," she said, her voice filled with quiet pride. "We broke free."

Dain nodded, his expression serious. "But the journey isn't over. We need to keep moving."

Lyra smiled, a hint of her usual confidence returning. "We've come this far, and we're not turning back now."

Breck grunted in agreement, his eyes filled with determination. "Aye, we've faced worse, and we'll face whatever comes next."

Tomas, though still shaken, managed a small smile. "We'll keep going. We have to."

With their minds clear and their purpose restored, the group left the oasis behind and continued their journey. The path ahead was uncertain, the challenges still daunting, but they had proven that they were capable of overcoming any obstacle, of resisting any temptation.

As they walked into the fading light of the day, the stars beginning to twinkle in the darkening sky, Elara felt a deep sense of hope and determination fill her heart. The journey ahead would be long and difficult, but they were stronger for the trials they had faced, and they were ready for whatever lay ahead.

Together, they would find the Mirror of Eldoria, fulfill the prophecy, and bring peace to the kingdom. They would face whatever challenges came their way, and they would do it as a team—united by the sacrifices they had made, and the bonds they had forged along the way.

And as they walked into the night, the future stretched out before them, filled with hope and promise.

END OF CHAPTER 9.

Chapter 10: The Mountain of Echoes

The morning air was crisp and clear as Elara and her companions continued their journey, leaving the deceptive oasis far behind. The trials they had faced so far had tested their resolve, their strength, and their unity. They had survived the Desert of Lost Time, resisted the temptations of the Enchanted Oasis, and now they were nearing the final leg of their journey. The Mirror of Eldoria, the object of their quest, was said to be hidden deep within the Mountain of Echoes—a place where the voices of past heroes could be heard, and where the path was fraught with dangers both physical and psychological.

As they approached the base of the mountain, its towering peaks loomed before them, shrouded in mist and shadow. The mountain was a formidable sight, its jagged cliffs rising high into the sky, disappearing into the clouds above. The air grew colder as they neared the mountain, a chill that seeped into their bones and made the task ahead seem even more daunting.

"We're almost there," Dain said, his voice steady but tinged with a sense of awe as he gazed up at the towering peaks. "The Mountain of Echoes."

Elara nodded, her heart pounding in her chest. The mountain was the final trial, the last obstacle standing between them and the Mirror of Eldoria. But it was also the most dangerous. The legends spoke of the mountain's treacherous paths, of the echoes that could drive even the bravest of souls to madness. The voices of past heroes could be heard within the mountain, whispering doubts and fears, challenging those who dared to seek the mirror.

"We need to be prepared," Elara said, her voice firm as she turned to her companions. "The climb will be difficult, and the echoes—whatever they are—will test us. We can't afford to let our guard down."

Lyra, who had always been quick with a quip or a smirk, was unusually quiet as she stared up at the mountain. "I've heard stories about this place," she said, her voice low. "The echoes... they say they can make you question everything you've ever believed. They bring out your deepest fears, your darkest doubts."

Breck, the burly blacksmith, grunted in agreement. "Aye, I've heard the same. But we've faced worse, haven't we? We'll get through this, same as we have with everything else."

Tomas, the healer's apprentice, looked pale but determined. "We've come too far to turn back now. Whatever the mountain throws at us, we'll face it together."

Elara felt a surge of pride for her companions. They had all been through so much, had faced dangers and challenges that would have broken lesser people. But they had stayed strong, had remained united in their quest. And now, they were so close to the end.

With a deep breath, Elara led the way toward the base of the mountain, her heart heavy with the weight of the task ahead. The path was steep and rocky, the ground uneven and treacherous underfoot. The wind howled around them, cold and biting, as if the mountain itself were warning them away.

The climb was slow and arduous, each step a struggle against the rugged terrain and the bitter cold. The higher they climbed, the thinner the air became, making it difficult to breathe, and the path grew narrower and more perilous. The mist that clung to the mountain was thick and heavy, obscuring their vision and making it difficult to see more than a few feet ahead.

But it wasn't just the physical challenges that weighed on Elara's mind. As they climbed higher, she began to hear faint whispers carried on the wind, voices that seemed to come from all around them, yet from nowhere at all. The voices were soft at first, barely audible over the sound of the wind and their labored breathing, but as they continued their ascent, the whispers grew louder, more insistent.

At first, Elara thought the voices were simply echoes of the wind, distorted by the mountain's strange acoustics. But as they climbed higher, the voices became clearer, more distinct, and she realized with a growing sense of unease that the whispers were not just random sounds, but words—words that seemed to be directed at them.

"You're not strong enough," one voice whispered, its tone filled with doubt.

"You'll never make it," another voice said, cold and cruel.

"Turn back now, before it's too late," a third voice urged, its tone filled with a sense of impending doom.

Elara shivered as the voices surrounded them, their words seeping into her mind, planting seeds of doubt and fear. She glanced at her companions, seeing the same unease reflected in their eyes. The echoes were starting to affect them, to worm their way into their thoughts, making them question their strength, their resolve.

But Elara knew they couldn't afford to give in to the doubts, to let the echoes weaken their resolve. They had come too far, had faced too many challenges, to turn back now. The Mirror of Eldoria was within their reach, and they couldn't let the mountain's whispers deter them.

"We have to keep moving," Elara said, her voice firm as she pushed forward, leading the way up the steep path. "Don't listen to the voices. They're trying to make us doubt ourselves, to turn us against each other. But we're stronger than that. We've faced worse, and we'll get through this."

Dain nodded, his expression resolute. "She's right. We can't let the echoes get to us. We have to stay focused, stay together."

Lyra took a deep breath, her eyes narrowing with determination. "Let them whisper all they want. We know what we're here for, and we're not turning back."

Breck grunted in agreement, his jaw set in a grim line. "Aye, we'll show this mountain what we're made of."

Tomas, though still visibly shaken, nodded as well. "We have to keep going. We can't let them win."

With renewed determination, the group pressed on, climbing higher and higher up the mountain. The path grew steeper and more treacherous, the ground slick with ice and loose rocks that threatened to send them tumbling down the mountainside. The wind howled around them, carrying the voices of the echoes, which grew louder and more insistent with every step they took.

"You're wasting your time," one voice whispered, its tone filled with bitterness.

"The mirror doesn't exist," another voice said, cold and mocking. "You're chasing a dream."

"You'll die up here," a third voice warned, its tone filled with a sense of finality. "Turn back now, before it's too late."

Elara gritted her teeth, trying to block out the voices, to focus on the task at hand. But the echoes were relentless, their whispers gnawing at her confidence, making her question everything she had believed in.

Was the mirror real? Was this quest worth the risks they had taken, the sacrifices they had made? Could they really succeed, or were they doomed to fail, to perish on this mountain like so many before them?

But even as the doubts gnawed at her mind, Elara forced herself to remember the lessons she had learned on this journey—the lessons of perseverance, of trust, of the strength that came from working together. They had faced countless challenges, had overcome seemingly insurmountable obstacles, and they had done so by relying on each other, by believing in their mission, in their purpose.

She knew that the echoes were trying to break them, to make them doubt themselves, but she also knew that they were stronger than that. They had to be.

"Don't listen to them," Elara said, her voice steady despite the fear that gnawed at her insides. "We've come this far because we believe in our mission, in each other. The echoes are trying to make us doubt that, but we can't let them win."

Dain, who was climbing just behind her, nodded in agreement. "We've faced worse than this. We've survived the desert, resisted the enchantment of the oasis. We can survive this, too."

Lyra, who was bringing up the rear, smiled grimly. "Let the echoes try to scare us. We know the truth—we know why we're here."

Breck, his face set in a determined scowl, grunted in agreement. "Aye, we'll see this through, no matter what."

Tomas, though still visibly shaken by the voices, nodded resolutely. "We'll get through this. Together."

With their resolve strengthened by each other's words, the group continued their ascent, the echoes growing louder and more frenzied as they climbed higher. The path was narrow and treacherous, the ground slick with ice and loose stones that threatened to give way under their feet. The wind howled around them, carrying the voices of the echoes, which now seemed to be coming from all directions, surrounding them in a cacophony of doubt and fear.

But Elara refused to let the echoes break her. She had learned too much, had come too far, to let the whispers of the past defeat her now. She knew that the voices were trying to exploit her deepest fears, to make her doubt herself and her companions, but she also knew that they were stronger than that.

As they climbed higher, the path grew steeper and more treacherous, the air thinning as they ascended into the clouds that clung to the mountain's peaks. The cold was biting, the wind relentless, but they pressed on, their determination unwavering.

And then, just as it seemed that the climb would never end, they reached a plateau—a flat, open space that stretched out before them, the ground covered in a thick layer of snow. The wind had died down, the air still and silent, and the voices of the echoes had faded into the background, leaving only a faint whisper on the edge of hearing.

Elara paused to catch her breath, her heart pounding in her chest as she gazed out at the plateau. The snow-covered ground was unbroken, pristine, as if no one had ever set foot on it before. The sky above was a pale, icy blue, the sun hidden behind a veil of clouds that cast a cold, diffuse light over the landscape.

"This must be it," Dain said, his voice low and tense as he joined Elara on the plateau. "The heart of the mountain."

Elara nodded, her gaze scanning the plateau for any sign of the Mirror of Eldoria. According to the legends, the mirror was hidden deep within the mountain, guarded by the spirits of past heroes—heroes whose voices could still be heard echoing through the peaks.

But as she looked around, she saw no sign of the mirror, no entrance to a hidden chamber, no clue as to where it might be. The plateau was empty, the snow unbroken, as if the mountain itself was hiding its secrets.

"Where is it?" Lyra asked, her voice tinged with frustration as she joined them on the plateau. "We've come all this way, and there's nothing here."

Breck grunted in agreement, his expression grim. "Aye, we've been climbing for hours, and there's no sign of the mirror. Are we sure this is the right place?"

Tomas, who was shivering from the cold, looked around with a worried expression. "What if the echoes were right? What if the mirror doesn't exist?"

Elara shook her head, refusing to let doubt take hold. "The mirror is here," she said, her voice filled with conviction. "We just have to find it."

But even as she said the words, she felt a flicker of uncertainty. The echoes had been relentless in their attempts to undermine their resolve, to make them doubt their mission. What if the mirror really didn't exist? What if this entire journey had been for nothing?

She pushed the doubts aside, focusing on the task at hand. The mirror was here—she had to believe that. They had come too far, had faced too many challenges, to give up now.

"Spread out," Elara said, her voice steady. "Search the plateau. There has to be something here, some clue to where the mirror is hidden."

The group nodded in agreement, each of them moving off in different directions to search the snow-covered plateau. The air was still and silent, the only sound the crunch of their footsteps on the snow as they searched for any sign of the mirror.

But as they searched, the echoes returned, their whispers growing louder, more insistent.

"It's not here," one voice said, cold and mocking.

"You've wasted your time," another voice whispered, filled with bitterness.

"You'll die up here, alone and forgotten," a third voice warned, its tone filled with a sense of finality.

Elara gritted her teeth, refusing to let the voices distract her. She knew the echoes were trying to break her, to make her doubt herself and her companions. But she also knew that they were stronger than that.

As she continued to search, her gaze fell on a patch of snow that seemed different from the rest—darker, almost as if the ground beneath it was hollow. She knelt down, brushing away the snow to reveal a stone slab, etched with strange symbols that seemed to glow faintly in the dim light.

"Over here!" Elara called out, her voice filled with excitement as she brushed away more of the snow to reveal the full extent of the stone slab. "I've found something!"

The others quickly joined her, their expressions filled with a mix of hope and anticipation as they gazed at the stone slab. The symbols etched into the stone were intricate and ancient, their meaning lost to time, but there was no doubt that this was a clue—perhaps even the entrance to the chamber where the mirror was hidden.

"How do we open it?" Lyra asked, her voice tinged with excitement as she examined the symbols.

Elara studied the stone slab, her mind racing as she tried to decipher the symbols. They were unlike anything she had ever seen before, but there was something familiar about them, something that tugged at the edge of her memory.

And then, with a sudden clarity, she remembered—the old sage, the man who had first told her of the prophecy. He had shown her a book, an ancient tome filled with the knowledge of the past, and within that book had been a passage about the Mountain of Echoes, about the ancient heroes who had guarded the mirror.

"The symbols," Elara said, her voice filled with realization. "They're a code, a puzzle. We have to solve it to open the entrance."

Dain frowned, his brow furrowed in concentration as he studied the symbols. "A code? How do we solve it?"

Elara's mind raced as she tried to recall the passage from the sage's book. The symbols were a key, a way to unlock the entrance to the chamber where the mirror was hidden. But the code was complex, designed to keep out those who were unworthy, those who were not meant to find the mirror.

"We have to align the symbols," Elara said, her voice steady as she reached out to touch the stone slab. "Each symbol represents a different aspect of the heroes who guarded the mirror—their courage, their wisdom, their strength. We have to align them in the right order to unlock the entrance."

The others nodded in understanding, their expressions filled with determination as they worked together to decipher the code. It was a complex puzzle, the symbols shifting and changing as they tried different combinations, but they refused to give up, their resolve unshaken.

As they worked, the echoes grew louder, more frenzied, their whispers filled with desperation and anger.

"You'll never solve it," one voice hissed, its tone filled with venom.

"You're wasting your time," another voice said, cold and mocking.

"Turn back now, before it's too late," a third voice warned, its tone filled with a sense of impending doom.

But Elara refused to let the voices distract her. She knew they were close, that they were on the verge of unlocking the entrance and finding the mirror. They had come too far, had faced too many challenges, to give up now.

Finally, after what felt like hours of trial and error, the symbols clicked into place, aligning perfectly to form a single, unified image—a glowing emblem that pulsed with a soft, golden light.

The ground beneath their feet trembled, the stone slab shifting and sliding to reveal a hidden staircase, descending deep into the heart of the mountain. The air was cold and still, the echoes fading into silence as the entrance to the chamber was revealed.

Elara felt a surge of relief and excitement as she gazed down the staircase, her heart pounding with anticipation. They had done it—they had unlocked the entrance, and the mirror was within their reach.

"We did it," Lyra said, her voice filled with awe as she stared at the entrance. "We found the way in."

Dain nodded, his expression serious but filled with a sense of accomplishment. "Now we just have to find the mirror."

Breck grunted in agreement, his eyes filled with determination. "Aye, let's finish this."

Tomas, though still visibly shaken by the echoes, managed a small smile. "We've come this far. Let's see it through."

With renewed determination, the group descended the staircase, the air growing colder and more oppressive as they ventured deeper into the heart of the mountain. The walls of the chamber were lined with ancient carvings, depicting scenes of battles and heroism, of the heroes who had once guarded the mirror.

The staircase led to a vast, circular chamber, the walls lined with torches that flickered with a cold, blue flame. At the center of the chamber stood a pedestal, and atop that pedestal was the Mirror of Eldoria.

The mirror was unlike anything Elara had ever seen—a large, ornate frame of gold and silver, encrusted with jewels that glowed with an inner light. The surface of the mirror was smooth and flawless, reflecting not just the physical world, but something deeper, something more profound.

Elara felt a sense of awe and reverence as she approached the mirror, her heart pounding in her chest. This was it—the object of their quest, the key to fulfilling the prophecy and bringing peace to the kingdom.

But as she reached out to touch the mirror, the echoes returned, their voices filled with a sense of finality.

"You are not worthy," one voice said, cold and cruel.

"The mirror does not belong to you," another voice whispered, filled with bitterness.

"You will fail," a third voice warned, its tone filled with a sense of impending doom.

Elara hesitated, the echoes' words gnawing at her resolve. But then she remembered the lessons she had learned on this journey—the lessons of perseverance, of trust, of the strength that came from working together. They had faced countless challenges, had overcome seemingly insurmountable obstacles, and they had done so by believing in each other, by believing in their mission.

With a deep breath, Elara reached out and touched the mirror, her fingers brushing the smooth, cold surface. The mirror glowed with a soft, golden light, the reflection shifting and changing to reveal not just the physical world, but the true nature of their quest—the sacrifices they had made, the bonds they had forged, the strength they had gained.

The echoes fell silent, their voices fading into the background as the mirror's light filled the chamber, illuminating the path forward.

Elara felt a sense of peace and clarity as she gazed into the mirror, her heart swelling with a deep, abiding knowledge that they had succeeded, that they were on the right path.

"We did it," she said softly, her voice filled with awe and reverence. "We found the mirror."

The others gathered around her, their expressions filled with a mix of relief and wonder as they gazed at the mirror. The journey had been long and difficult, the trials daunting and dangerous, but they had succeeded. They had found the Mirror of Eldoria, and now they were one step closer to fulfilling the prophecy.

As they stood together, the mirror's light shining brightly in the chamber, Elara felt a deep sense of hope and determination fill her heart. The journey ahead would still be challenging, the path uncertain, but they had proven that they were capable of overcoming any obstacle, of facing any trial.

Together, they would fulfill the prophecy, bring peace to the kingdom, and ensure that the sacrifices they had made, the bonds they had forged, were not in vain.

And as they prepared to leave the chamber, the mirror safely in their possession, Elara knew that they were stronger for the trials they had faced, and ready for whatever lay ahead.

End of Chapter 10.

Chapter 11: The Mirror's Keeper

The ascent to the peak of the Mountain of Echoes had been arduous, but Elara and her companions had overcome every obstacle. Now, with the Mirror of Eldoria safely in their possession, they stood at the mountain's summit, gazing out at the world below. The view was breathtaking—endless stretches of land, rivers winding like silver threads, and distant forests spreading out like a green tapestry. The sun was setting, casting the sky in hues of orange and pink, the clouds streaked with gold. It was a moment of triumph, a victory hard-earned after their long and difficult journey.

But the journey was not yet complete.

Elara held the Mirror of Eldoria in her hands, the surface gleaming with an otherworldly light. The mirror was heavy, not just in weight but in significance. It was said to hold the power to reveal one's true destiny, but as she gazed into its depths, Elara couldn't shake the feeling that the mirror held even more than that—something deeper, something far more profound.

"Do you feel that?" Lyra asked, her voice low as she looked around, her sharp eyes scanning the horizon. "It's like we're being watched."

Elara nodded, her grip tightening on the mirror. She felt it too—a presence, ancient and powerful, watching them from the shadows. The air was thick with magic, the very atmosphere humming with energy. It was as if the mountain itself was alive, aware of their presence and the significance of what they carried.

"We're not alone," Dain said, his voice tense as he drew his sword, his gaze sweeping over the rocky terrain. "Something's here with us."

Breck grunted in agreement, his hand resting on the hilt of his hammer. "Aye, and whatever it is, it doesn't feel friendly."

Tomas, the healer's apprentice, looked pale and nervous, his eyes wide with fear. "Do you think it's another trap? Another test?"

Elara didn't answer immediately. She could feel the presence growing stronger, the air around them thickening with anticipation. They had reached the summit, had found the mirror, but there was still one final trial to face—one last test that would determine if they were truly worthy of the mirror's power.

As if in response to her thoughts, the ground beneath their feet began to tremble, a deep rumbling that seemed to come from the very heart of the mountain. The wind picked up, howling through the peaks with a mournful wail that sent shivers down Elara's spine. The sky, once painted in the warm hues of sunset, darkened, clouds gathering overhead, swirling in a tumultuous vortex.

And then, from the shadows of the mountain, a figure emerged.

The being that stepped into the light was unlike anything Elara had ever seen. Tall and imposing, the figure was shrouded in a cloak of black, its form indistinct beneath the heavy fabric. The only part of the figure visible was its face—a pale, almost translucent visage with eyes that gleamed like twin stars, ancient and all-knowing. The being radiated power, an aura of timelessness that spoke of centuries, if not millennia, of existence.

Elara's breath caught in her throat as she met the gaze of the Mirror's Keeper. There was no doubt in her mind that this was the guardian of the Mirror of Eldoria, the ancient being who had watched over the mirror for countless generations.

"Who dares to claim the Mirror of Eldoria?" the Keeper's voice was deep and resonant, reverberating through the air like the tolling of a great bell. It was a voice filled with power and authority, one that demanded respect and obedience.

Elara stepped forward, her heart pounding in her chest, but her voice steady as she spoke. "I am Elara of Briar Glen, and these are my companions. We have journeyed far, faced many trials, to find the Mirror of Eldoria. We seek its power to fulfill the prophecy, to bring peace to the kingdom."

The Keeper's gaze swept over the group, its eyes lingering on each of them before returning to Elara. "You speak of prophecy, but do you truly understand the power you seek to wield? The Mirror of Eldoria is no mere tool to be used for your own ends. It is a mirror that reflects the truth of one's soul, revealing not just destiny, but the deepest, darkest parts of oneself."

Elara felt a chill run down her spine at the Keeper's words. She had known the mirror was powerful, but she hadn't fully grasped the extent of its power until now. The thought of facing the darkest parts of herself, of confronting the truths she had buried deep within, was terrifying.

The Keeper stepped closer, its gaze piercing. "To prove your worth, you must undergo a final test, Elara of Briar Glen. You must face the darkest parts of your soul, the fears and doubts that have plagued you, the shadows that have lingered in your heart. Only then will you be deemed worthy of the mirror's power."

Elara's heart pounded in her chest as the weight of the Keeper's words settled over her. She had faced many challenges on this journey, had confronted her fears and doubts time and again, but this was different. This was a test of her very soul, a trial that would force her to confront the darkest parts of herself, the parts she had tried to bury and forget.

But she knew she had no choice. If she wanted to fulfill the prophecy, to bring peace to the kingdom, she had to prove herself worthy of the mirror's power. She had to face the test.

"I accept the test," Elara said, her voice steady despite the fear that gnawed at her insides. "I will face whatever lies within."

The Keeper nodded, its expression inscrutable. "Very well. The test begins now."

With those words, the Keeper raised its hand, and the air around them seemed to shimmer and distort, as if reality itself was being twisted and reshaped. The world around Elara faded away, the mountain, her companions, even the Mirror of Eldoria, dissolving into nothingness.

When the world came back into focus, Elara found herself standing in a vast, empty space, the ground beneath her feet smooth and featureless, stretching out in all directions. The sky above was dark and stormy, lightning flashing in the distance, but there was no sound, no wind, no movement.

She was alone.

Elara's heart pounded in her chest as she looked around, trying to make sense of her surroundings. The emptiness was oppressive, the silence deafening. It was as if she had been transported to another realm, a place beyond time and space, where nothing existed but her and the test she was about to face.

And then, out of the darkness, a figure emerged.

Elara's breath caught in her throat as she recognized the figure—it was herself, but not as she was now. This was a younger version of herself, a girl of sixteen, with wide, innocent eyes and a hopeful smile. It was the Elara of her past, the girl she had once been before the prophecy had changed her life.

The younger Elara stepped forward, her expression filled with a mix of sadness and disappointment. "Why did you leave me behind?" she asked, her voice trembling with emotion. "Why did you forget who we were?"

Elara felt a pang of guilt as she met the gaze of her younger self. This was the girl she had been, the girl who had once believed in the simplicity of life, who had dreamed of a future filled with love and happiness. But that girl had been left behind, abandoned when Elara had taken up the mantle of the prophecy, when she had accepted the burden of her destiny.

"I didn't forget you," Elara said, her voice filled with regret. "But I had to move forward. I had to accept the prophecy, to fulfill my destiny."

The younger Elara shook her head, her eyes filling with tears. "But what about our dreams? What about the life we wanted? You gave it all up for a prophecy, for a destiny that you didn't choose. You left me behind."

Elara felt a lump form in her throat as she listened to the words of her younger self. It was true—she had given up her dreams, her hopes for a simple life, in order to fulfill the prophecy. But she had done so because she believed it was the right thing to do, because she believed in the greater good.

"I had to make a choice," Elara said, her voice filled with determination. "I chose to fight for something bigger than myself, to protect those I care about. It wasn't an easy choice, but it was the right one."

The younger Elara's expression softened, but the sadness in her eyes remained. "But at what cost? You've lost so much—your innocence, your hope, your belief in the goodness of the world. You've become hardened, closed off. Is this really who you want to be?"

Elara felt tears prick at the corners of her eyes as she listened to the words of her younger self. She had lost a part of herself along the way, had become someone who was focused on duty and responsibility, who had closed off her heart in order to protect herself from the pain of loss and disappointment.

But she also knew that she had gained something in return—strength, resilience, and a deeper understanding of the world and the people in it. She had learned to see beyond the surface, to recognize the complexities of life, and to find meaning in the struggles she had faced.

"I may have lost some things," Elara said softly, her voice filled with resolve. "But I've gained so much more. I've learned to be strong, to persevere in the face of adversity. I've learned to care deeply, to fight for what I believe in. And I've learned that even in the darkest times, there is always hope."

The younger Elara looked at her for a long moment, her expression thoughtful. Then, slowly, she nodded, a faint smile tugging at the corners of her lips. "Maybe you're right," she said softly. "Maybe you've become someone stronger, someone who can make a difference. But don't forget who you were, who we were. Don't forget the dreams we had, the love we felt. Hold on to that, even as you move forward."

Elara nodded, her heart swelling with a mix of emotions. "I won't forget," she promised. "I'll carry you with me, always."

The younger Elara smiled, her form beginning to fade into the darkness. "Goodbye, Elara," she said softly. "And good luck."

And with that, she was gone, leaving Elara alone once more in the empty, featureless space.

Elara took a deep breath, her heart heavy with the weight of the encounter. She had faced a part of herself she had long buried, had confronted the guilt and regret that had lingered in her heart. But she had also found a sense of closure, a resolution to carry with her as she continued her journey.

But the test was not over.

The ground beneath her feet began to tremble, the air around her growing thick with tension. The darkness that surrounded her seemed to close in, pressing down on her with a suffocating weight. And then, out of the darkness, another figure emerged.

This time, it was not a younger version of herself, but someone else—someone she had not seen in years. It was her mother, the woman she had lost so long ago, the woman whose death had left a wound in Elara's heart that had never fully healed.

Elara's breath caught in her throat as she gazed at the figure of her mother, her heart pounding with a mix of love, sorrow, and guilt. The woman before her looked just as she had in life—tall and graceful, with kind eyes and a warm smile. But there was a sadness in her gaze, a sorrow that seemed to reach deep into Elara's soul.

"Mother," Elara whispered, her voice trembling with emotion. "Is it really you?"

The woman smiled, but it was a sad smile, filled with a deep, abiding sorrow. "Elara, my dear," she said softly, her voice like a soothing balm. "It's been so long."

Elara felt tears well up in her eyes as she took a step forward, reaching out to touch her mother's hand. The warmth of her mother's touch was real, solid, grounding her in this moment.

"I've missed you so much," Elara whispered, her voice breaking. "I've tried to be strong, tried to move on, but I've never stopped missing you."

Her mother's smile softened, and she reached out to cup Elara's cheek, her touch gentle and comforting. "I know, my dear," she said softly. "I've watched over you, seen the strength and courage you've shown. You've grown into a remarkable young woman, Elara. I'm so proud of you."

Elara felt a tear slip down her cheek, her heart swelling with a mix of love and sorrow. "But I failed you," she said, her voice filled with regret. "I couldn't save you. I wasn't strong enough."

Her mother's expression grew serious, her gaze filled with understanding. "Elara, you were just a child," she said gently. "There was nothing you could have done. My death was not your fault."

Elara shook her head, her tears flowing freely now. "But I should have done more. I should have—"

Her mother placed a finger to her lips, silencing her. "Elara, listen to me," she said, her voice firm but filled with love. "You did everything you could. You were brave and strong, and you've carried that strength with you all these years. But you must learn to forgive yourself, to let go of the guilt that has weighed you down for so long."

Elara's heart ached with the truth of her mother's words, the pain of her loss still raw and unhealed. But as she looked into her mother's eyes, she felt a warmth spreading through her, a sense of peace and acceptance that she had not felt in years.

"I've missed you so much," Elara whispered, her voice filled with emotion. "I wish you were still here."

Her mother smiled, her eyes shining with love. "I'm always with you, Elara," she said softly. "In your heart, in your memories. I will always be with you."

Elara closed her eyes, allowing herself to feel the warmth of her mother's love, the peace that came with knowing she was not alone. She knew that this moment, this vision, was a gift from the Mirror's Keeper—a chance to confront her deepest regret, to find forgiveness and self-acceptance.

When she opened her eyes again, her mother was gone, the empty space around her fading into darkness. Elara felt a sense of loss, but also a sense of peace, a weight lifted from her shoulders.

The darkness around her began to shift and change, the ground beneath her feet solidifying as the world came back into focus. She was no longer in the empty, featureless space, but back on the mountain's peak, the Mirror of Eldoria still in her hands.

Her companions were with her, their expressions filled with concern and relief as they gathered around her.

"Elara, are you okay?" Dain asked, his voice filled with worry.

Elara nodded, her heart still heavy with the emotions of the test she had just faced. "I'm okay," she said softly. "I... I saw things. People from my past, from my memories. But I think... I think it was something I needed to face."

Lyra placed a hand on Elara's shoulder, her gaze filled with understanding. "Whatever you faced, you came through it. That's what matters."

Breck nodded in agreement, his expression serious. "Aye, you're stronger for it. We all are."

Tomas, though still pale and shaken, managed a small smile. "We're with you, Elara. Whatever comes next, we'll face it together."

Elara felt a surge of gratitude and love for her companions, the people who had stood by her through every trial, every challenge. They had faced the darkness of the forest, the dangers of the desert, the temptations of the oasis, and now the final test of the Mirror's Keeper. They had come through it all stronger, more united, and ready to face whatever lay ahead.

The Keeper stepped forward, its eyes gleaming with a strange, otherworldly light as it gazed at Elara. "You have faced the test of the mirror, Elara of Briar Glen," it said, its voice filled with a deep, resonant power. "You have confronted the darkest parts of your soul and emerged victorious. You are worthy of the mirror's power."

Elara felt a surge of relief and pride at the Keeper's words, but also a deep sense of humility. She had faced her fears, her doubts, and her regrets, and had come through stronger for it. But she also knew that this was just the beginning—that the journey ahead would still be challenging, the path uncertain.

"The mirror will reveal the truth of one's soul," the Keeper continued, its gaze sweeping over the group. "It is a powerful tool, but also a dangerous one. Use it wisely, and with great care. The truth it reveals may not always be easy to bear, but it is the truth nonetheless."

Elara nodded, her grip on the mirror tightening as she gazed into its depths. The surface of the mirror gleamed with an inner light, reflecting not just the world around them, but something deeper—something that spoke of destiny, of the soul, of the truths that lay hidden within.

"Thank you," Elara said softly, her voice filled with gratitude. "We will use the mirror wisely. We will fulfill the prophecy, and bring peace to the kingdom."

The Keeper nodded, its expression inscrutable. "Your journey is far from over, Elara of Briar Glen. The mirror has shown you the truth of your soul, but it is up to you to decide how to use that truth. The path ahead is fraught with danger, with trials yet to come. But you are strong, and you are not alone."

With those words, the Keeper stepped back, its form beginning to fade into the shadows. The air around them grew still, the tension that had hung over the mountain's peak lifting as the Keeper vanished into the darkness.

Elara took a deep breath, her heart filled with a mix of emotions—relief, gratitude, and a renewed sense of purpose. They had faced the Mirror's Keeper, had proven themselves worthy of the mirror's power, and now they were ready to continue their journey.

As they stood together on the mountain's peak, the world spread out before them, Elara felt a deep sense of hope and determination fill her heart. The journey ahead would still be challenging, the path uncertain, but they had proven that they were capable of overcoming any obstacle, of facing any trial.

Together, they would fulfill the prophecy, bring peace to the kingdom, and ensure that the sacrifices they had made, the bonds they had forged, were not in vain.

And as they prepared to descend the mountain, the Mirror of Eldoria safely in their possession, Elara knew that they were ready for whatever lay ahead.

End of Chapter 11.

Chapter 12: The Revelation

The descent from the Mountain of Echoes was a quiet one, the group of companions each lost in their thoughts. The encounter with the Mirror's Keeper had left them all feeling a strange mix of triumph and unease. They had gained the Mirror of Eldoria, the object of their quest, but they had also been warned of its power and the dangers that came with it.

As they made their way down the mountain's steep paths, the cold wind biting at their faces, Elara could feel the weight of the mirror in her pack like a physical burden. The mirror's power was undeniable, but so too was the responsibility that came with it. The Keeper's words echoed in her mind: *The mirror will reveal the truth of one's soul. Use it wisely, and with great care.*

Elara had always believed in the prophecy, had always known that her destiny was tied to the Mirror of Eldoria. But now, standing on the brink of fulfilling that destiny, she found herself questioning whether she was truly ready to face what the mirror would reveal. What if the truth was more than she could bear? What if it showed her something she didn't want to see?

But she also knew that she couldn't turn back now. They had come too far, faced too many challenges, to give up. The mirror was the key to bringing peace to the kingdom, to fulfilling the prophecy that had guided her for so long. She had to be strong, had to face whatever truths the mirror revealed, no matter how daunting.

As they reached the base of the mountain and entered the shelter of a small grove of trees, Elara called for them to stop. The grove was quiet and peaceful, a small clearing surrounded by ancient oaks and firs, their branches swaying gently in the wind. It was the perfect place to rest, to gather their strength before they continued their journey.

"We should take a moment," Elara said, her voice steady as she turned to her companions. "We've been through a lot, and we need to be ready for what comes next."

Dain nodded, his expression serious as he glanced around the clearing. "Aye, we could all use a rest."

Lyra, always practical, dropped her pack and began to rummage through it for supplies. "I'll set up camp. We should eat something, get our strength back."

Breck, the blacksmith, grunted in agreement as he began gathering wood for a fire. "A warm meal would do us all good."

Tomas, the healer's apprentice, looked pale and tired, but he managed a small smile as he joined Breck in building the fire. "We've come so far. It feels like we're finally close to the end."

Elara watched them work, her heart swelling with affection and gratitude for these people who had stood by her through everything. They had faced dangers together, had risked their lives for each other, and now they were closer than ever to fulfilling their mission. But she also knew that the hardest part was yet to come.

As the fire crackled to life and the smell of cooking food filled the air, Elara took a deep breath and reached into her pack, pulling out the Mirror of Eldoria. The mirror's surface gleamed in the firelight, its ornate frame catching the glow and casting flickering shadows across the ground.

The others fell silent as they saw the mirror, their eyes fixed on its shimmering surface. The mirror had been at the center of their journey, the goal they had fought so hard to reach, and now, finally, it was in their hands.

"We need to look into the mirror," Elara said, her voice steady but tinged with a sense of trepidation. "The Keeper said it would reveal the truth of our souls, our destinies. We need to know what it has to show us, so we can be ready for whatever comes next."

Dain's expression was serious as he nodded. "It's time. We've come this far—we need to see this through."

Lyra, always the skeptic, narrowed her eyes as she studied the mirror. "And what if we don't like what we see? What if the truth is something we can't handle?"

Elara met her gaze, her heart pounding in her chest. "Then we'll face it together, like we've faced everything else. We've been through too much to turn back now."

Breck grunted in agreement, his expression grim. "Aye, we'll face it. Whatever it is."

Tomas looked nervous, his hands trembling slightly as he gazed at the mirror. "Do you think... do you think it will change us? What if it shows us something that we can't come back from?"

Elara's heart ached at the fear in Tomas's voice, but she knew that they had no choice. The mirror was their only hope, the key to fulfilling the prophecy and bringing peace to the kingdom. They had to face whatever truths it revealed, no matter how difficult.

"We have to be strong," Elara said, her voice filled with determination. "We have to trust that the mirror will show us what we need to see, even if it's hard. This is our destiny—we can't turn away from it now."

With a deep breath, Elara placed the mirror on the ground in the center of the clearing, the firelight casting an eerie glow across its surface. The others gathered around her, their faces filled with a mix of fear, anticipation, and resolve.

Elara was the first to kneel before the mirror, her heart pounding in her chest as she gazed into its depths. The surface of the mirror was smooth and flawless, reflecting the world around it with perfect clarity. But as she stared into it, she felt something shift, as if the mirror were no longer just reflecting the physical world, but something deeper—something that lay within her own soul.

For a moment, there was nothing—just her own reflection staring back at her, her eyes wide with fear and uncertainty. But then, slowly, the image began to change.

The reflection of her face faded away, replaced by a swirling mist that seemed to rise up from the depths of the mirror. The mist was thick and heavy, obscuring everything, but as Elara watched, it began to clear, revealing a scene that took her breath away.

She saw herself standing on the edge of a great battlefield, the sky dark and stormy, the air filled with the sound of clashing swords and the cries of battle.

All around her, warriors fought with a ferocity born of desperation, their faces grim and determined as they fought for their lives, for their freedom.

And at the center of it all was Elara.

She stood tall and strong, her sword raised high, her eyes blazing with determination. She was a leader, a beacon of hope in the midst of the chaos, rallying her people to fight, to stand against the darkness that threatened to consume them all.

But there was something else—something darker, more ominous. As she watched, the scene shifted, the battlefield fading away to reveal a figure standing in the shadows, watching her with cold, calculating eyes.

The figure was tall and imposing, shrouded in darkness, its face obscured by a hood. But there was no mistaking the aura of power that radiated from it, an aura that sent a shiver down Elara's spine.

And then, as if sensing her presence, the figure turned its gaze on her, its eyes piercing through the darkness to lock onto hers. The eyes were cold, devoid of emotion, but there was a flicker of something else—something that sent a wave of fear crashing over her.

Hatred.

The figure hated her, and that hatred burned with an intensity that was almost palpable. It was a hatred that was personal, directed solely at her, and as she gazed into those eyes, Elara felt a chill run down her spine.

And then, just as suddenly as it had appeared, the image faded away, leaving her staring at her own reflection once more.

Elara's heart pounded in her chest as she pulled back from the mirror, her breath coming in short, ragged gasps. The vision had been so vivid, so real, that it had left her shaken to her core. She had seen her destiny, had seen the battles that lay ahead, but she had also seen the darkness that threatened to consume her.

"What did you see?" Dain asked, his voice filled with concern as he knelt beside her.

Elara shook her head, her mind racing as she tried to make sense of the vision. "I saw... a battlefield. A great war, with me at the center of it. I was leading our people, but there was something else—someone watching me, someone filled with hatred."

Lyra's eyes narrowed as she listened. "Hatred? Toward you?"

Elara nodded, her heart still pounding in her chest. "Yes. It was personal, directed at me. Whoever it was... they wanted to destroy me."

Breck grunted, his expression grim. "Sounds like we've got more enemies than we thought."

Tomas looked pale and shaken, his hands trembling as he gazed at the mirror. "And that's what we're supposed to face? A war?"

Elara took a deep breath, trying to steady her nerves. "The mirror showed me my destiny, but it also showed me the dangers that come with it. I don't know who that figure was, but I know that they're a threat—not just to me, but to all of us."

Dain placed a hand on her shoulder, his expression serious. "Whatever happens, we'll face it together. We've come this far—we can't turn back now."

Elara nodded, her heart swelling with gratitude for her companions. They had stood by her through everything,

had faced every challenge with courage and determination. She knew that whatever the future held, they would face it together.

But the mirror wasn't just for her. It held truths for each of them, and they all needed to see what it had to reveal.

"Who's next?" Elara asked, her voice steady despite the lingering fear that gnawed at her insides.

Lyra was the first to step forward, her expression resolute as she knelt before the mirror. She had always been the skeptic, the one who questioned everything, but now, as she gazed into the mirror's depths, Elara could see the flicker of uncertainty in her eyes.

For a moment, nothing happened—just Lyra's reflection staring back at her, her eyes narrowed with suspicion. But then, slowly, the image began to change, the mist rising up from the depths of the mirror to obscure her reflection.

The mist swirled and shifted, and then, as it cleared, a new scene was revealed.

Elara watched as Lyra's expression shifted, her eyes widening with shock as she saw what the mirror had to show her. Her lips parted as if to speak, but no words came out, her breath catching in her throat.

"What do you see?" Elara asked, her voice filled with concern.

Lyra shook her head, her eyes fixed on the mirror. "It's... it's not possible," she whispered, her voice trembling. "This can't be real."

Elara felt a surge of worry as she watched Lyra's reaction. Whatever the mirror was showing her, it was something that had shaken her to her core.

"What is it?" Dain asked, his voice filled with urgency. "What did you see?"

Lyra's hands clenched into fists, her knuckles white as she gazed into the mirror. "I saw... I saw myself," she said, her voice trembling. "But it wasn't me—not the me I know. It was someone else—someone cruel, someone heartless."

Elara's heart ached as she listened to Lyra's words. The mirror was showing them their deepest fears, their darkest truths, and it was clear that Lyra was struggling to come to terms with what she had seen.

"You're not cruel," Elara said softly, her voice filled with compassion. "You've always been strong, always fought for what you believe in."

Lyra shook her head, her eyes filled with a mix of fear and self-doubt. "But what if... what if that's who I'm becoming? What if the battles we've fought, the things we've had to do, are changing me?"

Elara reached out and took Lyra's hand, her grip firm and reassuring. "We've all changed, Lyra. We've had to make hard choices, had to do things we never thought we would. But that doesn't make us cruel or heartless. It makes us survivors."

Lyra's eyes filled with tears as she met Elara's gaze. "But what if I lose myself along the way? What if I become someone I don't recognize?"

Elara squeezed her hand, her voice filled with determination. "You won't. We won't let that happen. We'll stand by each other, no matter what."

Lyra nodded, her tears spilling over as she pulled back from the mirror. "I hope you're right," she whispered, her voice filled with uncertainty.

Dain was next, his expression grim as he knelt before the mirror. He had always been the protector, the one who stood at the front lines, ready to defend those he cared about. But as he gazed into the mirror's depths, Elara could see the flicker of doubt in his eyes.

The mist rose up from the mirror, obscuring Dain's reflection, and then, as it cleared, a new scene was revealed.

Elara watched as Dain's expression shifted, his eyes narrowing with a mix of anger and fear. His hands clenched into fists, his jaw set in a grim line as he stared into the mirror.

"What do you see?" Elara asked, her voice filled with concern.

Dain's voice was low and filled with tension as he spoke. "I see... failure," he said, his words clipped. "I see myself failing to protect the people I care about, failing to keep them safe."

Elara's heart ached as she listened to Dain's words. The mirror was showing him his deepest fears, the fear of failure, of not being able to protect those he loved.

"You've never failed us, Dain," Elara said softly, her voice filled with compassion. "You've always been there, always fought to keep us safe."

Dain shook his head, his expression filled with self-reproach. "But what if I do? What if there comes a time when I can't protect you, when I can't keep you safe?"

Elara reached out and placed a hand on his shoulder, her grip firm and reassuring. "We're in this together, Dain. You're not alone in this fight. We'll protect each other, no matter what."

Dain's expression softened, his eyes filled with a mix of gratitude and resolve. "You're right," he said softly. "We'll protect each other. We won't let fear control us."

Breck was the last to kneel before the mirror, his expression serious as he gazed into its depths. The burly blacksmith had always been a man of few words, but his strength and loyalty had been a constant source of support for the group.

The mist rose up from the mirror, obscuring Breck's reflection, and then, as it cleared, a new scene was revealed.

Elara watched as Breck's expression shifted, his brow furrowing with a mix of confusion and concern. He stared into the mirror, his eyes narrowing as he tried to make sense of what he was seeing.

"What is it?" Elara asked, her voice filled with concern.

Breck shook his head, his voice low and filled with uncertainty. "I see... a child," he said slowly. "A little girl. She's alone, crying."

Elara felt a pang of sadness as she listened to Breck's words. The mirror was showing him something deeply personal, something that had struck a chord in his heart.

"Do you know who she is?" Dain asked, his voice gentle.

Breck nodded slowly, his expression filled with sorrow. "She's my daughter," he said softly. "The daughter I lost years ago."

Elara's heart ached for Breck as she listened to his words. The mirror was showing him a painful truth, a reminder of the loss he had carried with him for so long.

"I couldn't save her," Breck continued, his voice trembling with emotion. "I couldn't protect her. And now... now I'm afraid that I'll lose all of you, too."

Elara reached out and took Breck's hand, her grip firm and reassuring. "We're not going anywhere, Breck," she said softly. "We're in this together, and we'll get through it together."

Breck's eyes filled with tears as he met Elara's gaze, his expression filled with a mix of gratitude and sorrow. "Thank you," he whispered, his voice filled with emotion. "Thank you for standing by me."

Elara squeezed his hand, her heart swelling with love and gratitude for her companions. They had faced so much together, had confronted their deepest fears and darkest truths, and now they were stronger for it.

As they sat together around the fire, the Mirror of Eldoria still glowing softly in the center of the clearing, Elara knew that they had reached a turning point. The mirror had shown them their destinies, their fears, and their truths, and now they had to decide whether to accept or reject what they had seen.

The path ahead was still uncertain, still filled with dangers and challenges, but Elara knew that they were ready for whatever came next. They had faced their fears, had confronted their doubts, and had emerged stronger for it.

Together, they would fulfill the prophecy, bring peace to the kingdom, and ensure that the sacrifices they had made, the bonds they had forged, were not in vain.

And as they sat together, the firelight casting flickering shadows across their faces, Elara knew that they were ready to face whatever destiny had in store for them.

End of Chapter 12.

Chapter 13: The Return Home

The dawn was breaking, the first light of day creeping over the horizon as Elara and her companions prepared to leave the grove where they had rested. The Mirror of Eldoria was safely tucked away in Elara's pack, but its presence weighed heavily on all of them. The revelations from the night before had shaken them, each of them having glimpsed the deepest parts of their souls. Now, as they began their journey home, the knowledge of what they had seen in the mirror lingered in their minds, a silent companion to their thoughts.

The journey back to their kingdom was long and arduous, the path winding through forests, across rivers, and over hills. The terrain was familiar, yet each step felt different, colored by the experiences and truths they now carried with them. The sun shone brightly, the sky a clear expanse of blue, but the atmosphere within the group was heavy with unspoken thoughts and unresolved emotions.

Elara led the way, her thoughts swirling as she tried to make sense of the vision the mirror had shown her. The battlefield, the war, the figure filled with hatred—these images haunted her, making her question the path that lay ahead. She had always known that her destiny was tied to the prophecy, but now she couldn't shake the feeling that the mirror had shown her a future that was far more daunting and perilous than she had ever imagined.

Dain walked beside her, his expression serious and thoughtful. He had always been the protector, the one who stood at the forefront of every battle, but the mirror had shown him his greatest fear—the fear of failure. The image of himself unable to protect those he cared about, of being powerless in the face of danger, had left him shaken. As they walked, he struggled with the weight of this new knowledge, trying to reconcile it with the man he had always believed himself to be.

Lyra followed a short distance behind them, her sharp eyes scanning the landscape, but her mind was elsewhere. The mirror had shown her a version of herself that she barely recognized—a woman who had become cruel and heartless, someone who had lost her way. The vision had left her questioning everything she had ever believed in, and now she struggled with the fear that she might lose herself along the way, that the battles they fought might change her in ways she couldn't control.

Breck brought up the rear, his usually stoic expression now clouded with sorrow. The mirror had shown him his daughter, the child he had lost so many years ago, a loss that had left a wound in his heart that had never fully healed. The vision had brought that pain back to the surface, reminding him of the fragility of life and the fear that he might lose those he cared about all over again.

Tomas, the healer's apprentice, walked quietly in the middle of the group, his thoughts turning over the vision the mirror had shown him. Unlike the others, his vision had been more abstract, a series of images and feelings that had left him confused and uncertain. He had seen himself standing at a crossroads, two paths stretching out before him—one bathed in light, the other shrouded in darkness. The vision had filled him with a sense of dread, as if the choice he made at that crossroads would determine not just his fate, but the fate of all those he cared about.

As they walked, the silence between them grew heavier, the weight of their new knowledge pressing down on them. They had faced so much together, had fought side by side through countless trials, but now they found themselves struggling with the consequences of what the mirror had revealed.

Elara could feel the tension in the group, the unspoken fears and doubts that lingered just beneath the surface. She knew that they couldn't continue like this, that they needed to confront what they had seen in the mirror, to find a way to come to terms with it. But she also knew that it wasn't something that could be forced, that each of them needed to find their own way to deal with the knowledge they had gained.

It was Dain who broke the silence first, his voice low and filled with tension as he spoke. "We need to talk about what we saw," he said, his gaze fixed on the path ahead. "We can't just pretend it didn't happen."

Elara nodded, her heart heavy with the weight of her own thoughts. "I know," she said softly. "But it's not easy. What the mirror showed us... it was personal, painful. We need to give each other time to process it."

Lyra let out a bitter laugh, her voice laced with frustration. "Time? What good is time when all it does is make you doubt yourself? I thought I knew who I was, but now... I'm not so sure."

Breck grunted in agreement, his expression grim. "Aye, the mirror didn't exactly show us the best parts of ourselves. It's hard to come to terms with that."

Tomas, who had been silent until now, spoke up, his voice trembling with uncertainty. "What if... what if the mirror showed us what we're meant to avoid? What if it's a warning, not a prophecy?"

Elara considered his words, her mind turning over the possibilities. The mirror was powerful, but it was also enigmatic, its true nature difficult to understand. What if Tomas was right? What if the visions they had seen were not set in stone, but warnings of what could happen if they strayed from the path?

"We can't know for sure," Elara said finally, her voice steady. "But we do have a choice. We can let what we saw control us, let it fill us with fear and doubt. Or we can use it as a guide, a reminder of what we need to avoid, of what we need to fight against."

Dain nodded, his expression thoughtful. "Maybe you're right. Maybe the mirror was showing us the dangers ahead, the challenges we'll face. But that doesn't mean we're powerless. We can still choose how we respond to it."

Lyra's gaze softened, her frustration giving way to a sense of resolve. "We've faced worse than this," she said quietly. "We've always found a way to get through it, together."

Breck's expression remained grim, but there was a flicker of determination in his eyes. "We've got each other. That's something, at least."

Tomas managed a small smile, though it was tinged with uncertainty. "We'll figure it out. We always do."

Elara felt a surge of hope as she listened to her companions' words. They were struggling, yes, but they were also finding strength in each other, in the bonds they had forged over the course of their journey. The mirror had shown them their darkest fears, but it had also given them a chance to confront those fears, to find a way to overcome them.

As they continued their journey, the mood among the group began to lighten, the tension slowly easing as they talked about what they had seen in the mirror, about their fears and doubts. It wasn't easy—there were still moments of silence, of uncertainty—but they were starting to find their way forward, to come to terms with the knowledge they had gained.

The days passed slowly as they made their way back to the kingdom, the landscape changing around them as they traveled. The forests gave way to rolling hills, the rivers to wide plains, and the air grew warmer as they descended from the mountains.

Elara found herself thinking more and more about the vision the mirror had shown her, about the battlefield and the figure filled with hatred. She couldn't shake the feeling that the figure was more than just a threat—it was a part of her destiny, a challenge she would have to face head-on.

But she also knew that she wasn't alone. Her companions were with her, and together they had faced dangers and challenges that would have broken lesser people. They had come through it all stronger, more united, and ready for whatever lay ahead.

One evening, as they made camp near the edge of a forest, Dain approached Elara, his expression serious. "Can we talk?" he asked, his voice low.

Elara nodded, motioning for him to sit beside her by the fire. The others were busy setting up camp, their voices murmuring softly in the background, but Elara could sense that Dain had something important on his mind.

"What is it?" Elara asked, her voice gentle.

Dain took a deep breath, his gaze fixed on the flames as he spoke. "I've been thinking a lot about what the mirror showed me," he said, his voice filled with tension. "About the fear of failure, of not being able to protect the people I care about."

Elara listened quietly, her heart aching for him. Dain had always been the protector, the one who took on the heaviest burdens to keep others safe. The fear of failure was something that weighed on him more than anyone else, and the mirror had brought that fear to the forefront.

"I've always prided myself on being strong, on being able to stand up to any challenge," Dain continued, his voice trembling slightly. "But what if I'm not strong enough? What if there comes a time when I can't protect you, when I can't keep any of you safe?"

Elara reached out and placed a hand on his shoulder, her grip firm and reassuring. "You've always been there for us, Dain," she said softly. "You've protected us through every danger, every battle. But you're not alone in this. We're in this together, and we'll protect each other."

Dain's gaze softened as he looked at her, a small smile tugging at the corners of his lips. "I know," he said quietly. "But it's hard to let go of that fear. It's always been a part of who I am."

Elara nodded, her heart heavy with empathy. "We all have our fears, Dain. But we don't have to face them alone. We have each other, and that's what makes us strong."

Dain's smile widened, and he reached out to take her hand, squeezing it gently. "Thank you, Elara," he said softly. "For everything."

Elara smiled back, her heart swelling with affection for the man who had stood by her through so much. "We'll get through this, Dain. Together."

As the fire crackled softly in the background, the two of them sat in companionable silence, the weight of their fears easing as they found comfort in each other's presence.

The next day, as they continued their journey, Lyra pulled Elara aside, her expression thoughtful. "I've been thinking about what Tomas said," she said quietly. "About the mirror's vision being a warning, not a prophecy."

Elara nodded, her mind already turning over the possibilities. "It makes sense," she said. "The mirror showed us what could happen if we're not careful, if we let fear and doubt control us."

Lyra's gaze was serious as she met Elara's eyes. "I've always prided myself on being strong, on not letting anything get to me. But the mirror showed me something... something that scared me. I don't want to become that person, Elara. I don't want to lose myself."

Elara reached out and took Lyra's hand, her voice filled with compassion. "You're stronger than you think, Lyra. You've always fought for what's right, always stood up for what you believe in. That's who you are, and that's who you'll continue to be."

Lyra's eyes filled with tears as she squeezed Elara's hand. "Thank you," she whispered, her voice trembling. "I needed to hear that."

Elara smiled, her heart swelling with affection for the woman who had become like a sister to her. "We'll get through this, Lyra. We'll face whatever comes next, and we'll do it together."

As the days passed and the landscape around them grew more familiar, the group began to find their footing again, the weight of the mirror's revelations easing as they talked through their fears and doubts. They were still haunted by what they had seen, still struggling with the knowledge they had gained, but they were also finding strength in each other, in the bonds they had forged over the course of their journey.

One evening, as they camped by a river, Breck approached Elara, his expression somber. "I've been thinking about what the mirror showed me," he said quietly, his voice heavy with emotion.

Elara nodded, her heart aching for him. Breck had always been the quiet, steady presence in the group, the one who never let his emotions show. But the mirror had revealed a deep, lingering pain that he had carried with him for years—the loss of his daughter.

"It brought back memories I thought I'd buried," Breck continued, his voice trembling slightly. "The pain of losing her, the fear that I might lose all of you, too. It's been hard to come to terms with that."

Elara reached out and placed a hand on his shoulder, her voice filled with compassion. "You're not alone, Breck," she said softly. "We're all in this together. And we're not going anywhere."

Breck's eyes filled with tears as he looked at her, his expression filled with gratitude. "Thank you, Elara," he said quietly. "For standing by me."

Elara smiled, her heart swelling with affection for the man who had become like a brother to her. "We'll get through this, Breck. Together."

As the fire crackled softly in the background, the two of them sat in companionable silence, the weight of their fears easing as they found comfort in each other's presence.

The days passed, the group slowly making their way back to the kingdom. The landscape around them grew more familiar, the sights and sounds of home drawing closer with each passing day. But as they neared the kingdom's borders, the weight of the mirror's revelations began to settle over them once more, a reminder of the challenges that still lay ahead.

Elara knew that the journey was far from over. They had faced their fears, had confronted their darkest truths, but now they had to decide whether to accept or reject what the mirror had shown them. The path ahead was uncertain, the dangers still looming, but they were stronger for the trials they had faced, and they were ready for whatever came next.

One evening, as they camped near the edge of a forest, Tomas approached Elara, his expression filled with uncertainty. "Can we talk?" he asked, his voice trembling slightly.

Elara nodded, motioning for him to sit beside her by the fire. The others were busy setting up camp, their voices murmuring softly in the background, but Elara could sense that Tomas had something important on his mind.

"What is it?" Elara asked gently.

Tomas took a deep breath, his gaze fixed on the flames as he spoke. "The mirror showed me something... something I don't fully understand," he said quietly. "I saw myself standing at a crossroads, with two paths stretching out before me—one bathed in light, the other shrouded in darkness."

Elara listened quietly, her heart aching for the young man who had become like a younger brother to her. The vision the mirror had shown him was abstract, but its implications were clear—Tomas was facing a choice, one that would determine not just his fate, but the fate of all those he cared about.

"I don't know what it means," Tomas continued, his voice trembling with uncertainty. "I don't know which path to choose, or what the consequences will be."

Elara reached out and took his hand, her grip firm and reassuring. "We don't always know what the right choice is, Tomas," she said softly. "But we have to trust ourselves, trust our instincts. Whatever choice you make, know that we'll stand by you, no matter what."

Tomas's eyes filled with tears as he squeezed her hand, his expression filled with gratitude. "Thank you, Elara," he whispered, his voice trembling. "I don't know what I'd do without you."

Elara smiled, her heart swelling with affection for the young man who had become like family to her. "We'll get through this, Tomas. Together."

As the fire crackled softly in the background, the two of them sat in companionable silence, the weight of their fears easing as they found comfort in each other's presence.

The next morning, as they prepared to continue their journey, Elara felt a renewed sense of resolve. They had faced their fears, had confronted their darkest truths, and now they were ready to face whatever came next. The mirror had shown them their destinies, but it was up to them to decide how they would respond to that knowledge, how they would shape their futures.

As they crossed the final river and entered the borders of the kingdom, the sun was setting, casting the sky in hues of orange and pink. The sight of their homeland, so familiar and yet so distant after all they had been through, filled Elara with a sense of both nostalgia and anticipation. They had returned home, but they were not the same people who had left on this journey.

The kingdom was still at peace, the villagers going about their daily lives, unaware of the trials that had been faced, the battles that had been fought to protect them. Elara knew that the true battle was still to come, that the prophecy was yet to be fulfilled, but she also knew that they were ready for it. They had faced their fears, had confronted their darkest truths, and they were stronger for it.

As they entered the gates of the capital, the city bathed in the warm glow of the setting sun, Elara felt a sense of calm settle over her. They had returned home, but the journey was far from over. The Mirror of Eldoria was safe in her possession, its power a reminder of the challenges that still lay ahead. But she also knew that they were ready to face those challenges, that they were stronger for the trials they had faced.

Together, they would fulfill the prophecy, bring peace to the kingdom, and ensure that the sacrifices they had made, the bonds they had forged, were not in vain.

And as they walked through the city streets, the future stretched out before them, filled with hope and promise.

End of Chapter 13.

Chapter 14: The Final Confrontation

The kingdom's capital city buzzed with life as Elara and her companions made their way through the crowded streets, the golden light of the setting sun casting long shadows across the cobblestones. The familiarity of the surroundings—once so comforting—now felt strangely alien, as if the journey they had been on had changed not just them, but the world around them. The Mirror of Eldoria, tucked securely in Elara's pack, was a heavy reminder of the task that lay ahead.

For days, Elara had felt an uneasy tension building within her. The return home had been a long-awaited relief, yet the weight of the prophecy and the mirror's revelations had not lifted. Instead, it had grown heavier, pressing down on her with the knowledge that their true challenge was still ahead. The visions the mirror had shown them—of war, of hatred, of choices that could change everything—were no longer just possibilities. They were fast becoming reality.

Elara's thoughts turned to the vision that had haunted her since she first gazed into the mirror—the dark figure standing on the battlefield, eyes burning with an intense hatred directed solely at her. She had no doubt that this figure was their true enemy, the one who had been manipulating events from the shadows, pulling the strings that had led them to this point. But who was this enemy, and why did they harbor such hatred for her?

As they approached the palace gates, the imposing stone walls looming before them, Elara felt a shiver of apprehension run down her spine. The capital was peaceful, the people going about their lives as if nothing was amiss, but she knew better. There was a darkness here, lurking just beneath the surface, waiting for the right moment to strike.

"We need to be ready," Dain said quietly as they reached the gates, his hand resting on the hilt of his sword. "Whatever happens, we have to stay together."

Elara nodded, her heart pounding in her chest. "We've faced everything together so far. We won't stop now."

Lyra, ever the pragmatist, scanned the area with sharp eyes, her hand resting on the dagger at her belt. "I don't like this," she muttered. "It's too quiet. Something's not right."

Breck grunted in agreement, his expression grim. "Aye, there's a storm coming. I can feel it in my bones."

Tomas, the youngest of the group, looked pale but determined as he adjusted the strap of his pack. "We'll face it together," he said, his voice trembling slightly. "Whatever comes, we'll get through it."

The guards at the gate recognized them immediately and allowed them entry without question, though Elara noticed the wary looks they exchanged as the group passed through the archway. It was clear that the news of their journey—and the prophecy—had spread, and that the people of the kingdom were both hopeful and fearful of what was to come.

The palace courtyard was bustling with activity, servants and soldiers moving about with a sense of urgency that mirrored the tension Elara felt in the air. As they approached the grand entrance to the palace, the heavy wooden doors swung open, revealing a tall, stern-faced man in ornate armor—Lord Garrick, the king's most trusted advisor.

"Welcome back, Elara," Lord Garrick said, his voice deep and resonant. "The king has been awaiting your return. He will be relieved to know that you have succeeded in your quest."

Elara inclined her head in greeting, though her gaze remained sharp as she studied the man before her. Lord Garrick had always been a loyal servant of the crown, a man of honor and integrity, but there was something in his eyes now that made her uneasy—something dark and calculating.

"Thank you, Lord Garrick," Elara replied, her voice steady. "We have much to discuss with the king. The journey was long, and we have uncovered many truths."

Lord Garrick's expression remained inscrutable as he stepped aside, motioning for them to enter the palace. "The king is in the throne room. He has been preparing for your return. Please, follow me."

Elara exchanged a quick glance with Dain, who gave her a slight nod of reassurance. They had to be careful—whatever was happening here, they couldn't afford to let their guard down.

As they followed Lord Garrick through the grand halls of the palace, Elara couldn't shake the feeling that they were walking into a trap. The walls, once adorned with banners and tapestries celebrating the kingdom's victories, now felt cold and foreboding, the shadows seeming to stretch longer as they passed. The servants they encountered along the way were silent and tense, their eyes downcast as if afraid to meet her gaze.

When they finally reached the massive doors of the throne room, Lord Garrick paused, turning to face them with a grave expression. "The king is eager to hear of your success," he said, his tone measured. "But I must warn you—things have changed since you left. The kingdom is on the brink of war, and the decisions we make now will determine the fate of us all."

Elara's heart skipped a beat at his words, but she forced herself to remain calm. "We understand, Lord Garrick. We are prepared for whatever comes."

Lord Garrick's eyes narrowed slightly as he studied her, as if searching for something in her expression. Then, with a curt nod, he pushed open the doors, revealing the vast throne room beyond.

The throne room was as grand as Elara remembered, with towering pillars of marble and a high, vaulted ceiling that seemed to stretch up to the heavens. The floor was polished to a mirror-like sheen, reflecting the light from the massive chandeliers that hung above. At the far end of the room, seated on a golden throne, was King Alaric, his regal presence commanding the attention of everyone in the room.

But it was not the king who caught Elara's attention—it was the figure standing beside him.

Dressed in dark robes, their face obscured by a deep hood, the figure exuded an aura of power and malevolence that made Elara's blood run cold. The very air around them seemed to shimmer with dark energy, and Elara knew, with a sinking feeling in her gut, that this was the person from her vision—the figure filled with hatred, the one who had been manipulating events from the shadows.

The true antagonist.

"Your Majesty," Elara said, her voice steady despite the fear that gnawed at her insides. "We have returned, as you requested. The Mirror of Eldoria is in our possession."

King Alaric's gaze softened as he looked at her, his expression filled with a mix of relief and hope. "Elara, you have done a great service to the kingdom. The prophecy is near its fulfillment, and with the mirror's power, we can finally secure peace for our people."

But before Elara could respond, the figure beside the king stepped forward, their voice cold and commanding as they spoke. "Peace is a fragile thing, Your Majesty. And it is not always achieved through prophecy or power."

The figure's words sent a chill down Elara's spine, and she could feel the tension in the room heighten as the other members of her group braced themselves for what was to come.

"Who are you?" Elara demanded, her voice firm as she stepped forward, her gaze fixed on the figure. "And why are you here?"

The figure chuckled, a low, sinister sound that echoed through the throne room. "I am the one who has guided you on this path, Elara. The one who has watched and waited, shaping the events that have led you here. You have seen me in your visions, felt my presence in the shadows. I am the Keeper of the Dark Mirror, and I have been waiting for this moment for a long time."

Elara's heart pounded in her chest as the figure's words sank in. The Dark Mirror—an ancient artifact said to be the twin of the Mirror of Eldoria, but with a power that was the exact opposite. While the Mirror of Eldoria revealed the truth of one's soul, the Dark Mirror was said to corrupt, to twist the truth into lies, to turn light into darkness.

"You've been manipulating us," Dain said, his voice filled with anger as he drew his sword. "You've been pulling the strings from the shadows, leading us into this trap."

The Keeper of the Dark Mirror laughed again, the sound filled with dark amusement. "Oh, Dain, always so quick to draw your weapon. But this is not a battle that can be won with swords. This is a battle of wills, of destiny."

Elara's mind raced as she tried to make sense of what was happening. The Keeper of the Dark Mirror had been guiding them all along, manipulating events to bring them to this moment. But why? What was the Keeper's goal, and what did they hope to achieve by pitting the Mirror of Eldoria against the Dark Mirror?

"You seek to use the Mirror of Eldoria to fulfill the prophecy," the Keeper continued, their voice filled with dark intent. "But you do not understand the true nature of the prophecy, nor the power you hold in your hands. The Mirror of Eldoria is not a tool of light—it is a tool of balance, of truth. And with the Dark Mirror in my possession, I can twist that truth, bend it to my will."

Elara's heart sank as the Keeper's words hit home. The Mirror of Eldoria was powerful, but it was also vulnerable to corruption, to the influence of the Dark Mirror. The prophecy she had believed in for so long, the destiny she had fought to fulfill, was now in jeopardy, threatened by the very power she had sought to wield.

"We won't let you do this," Elara said, her voice filled with determination. "We won't let you corrupt the mirror or the prophecy. We will fight you, and we will win."

The Keeper's eyes gleamed with dark amusement as they spread their hands, the air around them crackling with dark energy. "Then let the battle begin, Elara. Let us see if you are truly worthy of the destiny you seek to claim."

The tension in the room reached a boiling point as the battle lines were drawn, the fate of the kingdom hanging in the balance. Elara could feel the weight of the Mirror of Eldoria in her pack, its power humming beneath the surface, but she knew that this battle would not be won with the mirror alone. This was a battle of wills, of strength and determination, and she would need all of her companions by her side if they were to have any hope of victory.

As the Keeper of the Dark Mirror raised their hands, a wave of dark energy surged through the room, the very air shimmering with its malevolent force. Elara and her companions braced themselves, drawing their weapons and preparing for the fight of their lives.

The battle that followed was unlike anything Elara had ever experienced. The Keeper of the Dark Mirror wielded their power with a terrifying precision, the dark energy twisting and warping the very fabric of reality around them. The walls of the throne room seemed to shift and distort, the floor rippling like water as the Keeper's power threatened to tear the world apart.

Elara fought with everything she had, her sword flashing in the dim light as she parried and struck, her movements guided by the training she had undergone for years. But no matter how hard she fought, the Keeper seemed to anticipate her every move, their dark energy countering her attacks with a frightening ease.

Dain was at her side, his swordsmanship as precise and deadly as ever, but even he was struggling to keep up with the Keeper's relentless onslaught. Breck swung his hammer with all his strength, each blow sending shockwaves through the room, but the Keeper's power seemed to absorb the impact, twisting it into something darker, something more dangerous.

Lyra moved with the grace of a shadow, her daggers flashing as she struck from the shadows, but the Keeper's senses were sharp, their every move countered with a wave of dark energy. Tomas, though not as skilled in combat as the others, used his knowledge of healing and protection to shield his friends, but even his spells were struggling to hold back the tide of darkness.

As the battle raged on, Elara could feel her strength waning, the weight of the Mirror of Eldoria growing heavier with each passing moment. The Keeper's power was overwhelming, their will unyielding, and Elara knew that if they continued like this, they would not survive.

But she also knew that this was not just a physical battle. The Keeper had said as much—this was a battle of wills, of destiny. The Mirror of Eldoria and the Dark Mirror were two sides of the same coin, and if Elara wanted to win, she would have to understand that balance, that truth.

As the Keeper launched another wave of dark energy at her, Elara ducked and rolled to the side, narrowly avoiding the blast. Her heart pounded in her chest as she searched for a way to turn the tide, to use the mirror's power to counter the Keeper's darkness.

And then it hit her.

The Mirror of Eldoria was a tool of truth, of balance. It revealed not just one's destiny, but the truth of one's soul. The Keeper of the Dark Mirror sought to twist that truth, to bend it to their will, but the truth was not something that could be controlled or corrupted. The truth was immutable, unchangeable, and it was the key to defeating the Keeper.

"Elara!" Dain shouted, his voice filled with urgency as he fought off another wave of dark energy. "We can't keep this up! We need to find a way to stop them!"

Elara's mind raced as she tried to formulate a plan, her heart pounding with the weight of the realization she had just come to. The Mirror of Eldoria was not just a weapon—it was a mirror, a reflection of the truth. And if she could find a way to use that truth against the Keeper, she might just have a chance.

"We need to use the mirror!" Elara shouted back, her voice filled with determination. "It's the key! The Keeper can't corrupt the truth if we reveal it for what it is!"

Dain's eyes widened as he realized what she was saying. "You're right! But how do we do it?"

Elara took a deep breath, her mind racing as she searched for a way to put her plan into action. The Keeper's power was formidable, but it was based on deception, on twisting the truth into something darker. If they could force the Keeper to confront the truth, to see their own reflection in the Mirror of Eldoria, they might be able to break their hold on the Dark Mirror.

"We need to get close!" Elara shouted, her voice filled with resolve. "We need to get the mirror in front of the Keeper, force them to see the truth!"

Dain nodded, his expression filled with determination. "I'll cover you! Get ready!"

With a fierce battle cry, Dain charged at the Keeper, his sword flashing as he drew their attention. The Keeper's dark energy surged toward him, but Dain was quick, dodging and weaving as he closed the distance between them.

Elara seized the opportunity, pulling the Mirror of Eldoria from her pack and holding it close as she moved toward the Keeper. The mirror's surface gleamed with an inner light, the truth it held within shining through even the darkest shadows.

Lyra and Breck moved in tandem with Dain, striking from the sides to keep the Keeper off balance, while Tomas used his magic to shield them from the worst of the dark energy. It was a desperate gamble, but it was their only hope.

As Elara neared the Keeper, she could feel the mirror's power humming beneath the surface, its light growing brighter as it neared its counterpart, the Dark Mirror. The air crackled with tension, the two mirrors' energies clashing in a battle of light and darkness.

The Keeper's eyes widened as they realized what Elara was doing, their expression twisting into one of rage and fear. "No!" they screamed, their voice filled with fury as they unleashed a torrent of dark energy. "You will not stop me!"

But it was too late. With a final burst of speed, Elara thrust the Mirror of Eldoria forward, its surface glowing with a brilliant light as it reflected the Keeper's image back at them.

The effect was immediate. The Keeper's dark energy faltered, their power wavering as they stared into the mirror, their own reflection staring back at them. The truth of who they were, of what they had become, was laid bare before them, and the Dark Mirror's power began to crumble under the weight of that truth.

"No..." the Keeper whispered, their voice trembling with fear as the dark energy around them began to dissipate. "This can't be... I am power... I am destiny..."

But the truth could not be denied. The Mirror of Eldoria's light continued to shine, reflecting the Keeper's soul for what it truly was—twisted, corrupted, and consumed by darkness. And as the Keeper confronted that truth, their power began to unravel, the Dark Mirror's energy fading into nothingness.

With a final, desperate scream, the Keeper's form disintegrated, the dark energy that had surrounded them dissipating into the air. The throne room fell silent, the echoes of the battle fading away as the Keeper was no more.

Elara collapsed to her knees, the Mirror of Eldoria still glowing softly in her hands. The battle was over, the truth had prevailed, but the cost had been great. She felt a wave of exhaustion wash over her, the weight of everything they had been through finally catching up with her.

Dain was at her side in an instant, his expression filled with concern as he knelt beside her. "Elara, are you alright?"

Elara managed a weak smile, her heart heavy with the weight of what they had just accomplished. "I'm alright," she said softly. "It's over. We did it."

Lyra and Breck joined them, their expressions a mix of relief and exhaustion as they surveyed the aftermath of the battle. Tomas stood a short distance away, his hands trembling as he stared at the spot where the Keeper had stood.

"We won," Lyra said quietly, her voice filled with a mix of disbelief and relief. "We actually won."

Breck grunted in agreement, his expression grim. "Aye, but it wasn't easy. That was too close."

Tomas finally tore his gaze away from the spot where the Keeper had vanished, his eyes wide with a mix of fear and awe. "The mirror... it really is that powerful, isn't it?"

Elara nodded, her heart heavy with the weight of the truth the mirror had revealed. "It is," she said softly. "But it's also a reminder that the truth is not something to be taken lightly. It's powerful, yes, but it's also dangerous. We have to be careful how we use it."

King Alaric, who had been watching the entire confrontation in stunned silence, finally stepped forward, his expression filled with a mix of relief and gratitude. "Elara, you have saved the kingdom," he said, his voice filled with emotion. "I cannot thank you enough for what you have done."

Elara shook her head, her heart heavy with the knowledge of what they had just faced. "

It wasn't just me, Your Majesty," she said softly. "We all fought together, and we all paid a price. The Keeper may be gone, but the truth of what we've seen, of what we've done, will stay with us."

The king nodded, his expression somber as he placed a hand on Elara's shoulder. "You have done a great service to the kingdom, Elara. The prophecy is fulfilled, and peace can finally be achieved. But you are right—the truth is not something that can be easily forgotten."

As the reality of what they had just accomplished settled over them, Elara felt a wave of relief wash over her. The battle was over, the threat of the Dark Mirror had been vanquished, and the kingdom was safe. But the cost had been high, and the memories of what they had faced would stay with them for the rest of their lives.

Together, Elara and her companions had faced their darkest fears, had confronted the truth of their souls, and had emerged victorious. They had fulfilled the prophecy, had brought peace to the kingdom, but they had also learned that the truth was not always easy to bear.

As they stood together in the throne room, the Mirror of Eldoria still glowing softly in Elara's hands, they knew that their journey was not truly over. The truth they had uncovered, the bonds they had forged, and the sacrifices they had made would continue to shape their destinies for years to come.

But for now, they had earned their victory. They had faced the darkness and had emerged into the light, stronger and more united than ever before.

And as they looked out at the kingdom they had fought so hard to protect, they knew that, whatever the future held, they would face it together.

End of Chapter 14.

Chapter 15: The Fulfillment of the Prophecy

The night sky was clear and filled with stars, a vast tapestry of light that stretched endlessly across the heavens. The air was cool and crisp, carrying with it the scent of pine and earth, and the only sound was the gentle rustling of leaves in the wind. The kingdom, for so long under the shadow of uncertainty, was now bathed in a peaceful calm that had not been felt in many years.

Elara stood at the edge of a small clearing in the forest, the Mirror of Eldoria cradled gently in her hands. The events of the past days weighed heavily on her mind—the battle against the Keeper of the Dark Mirror, the revelation of the truth, and the hard-won victory that had saved the kingdom. The mirror, its surface gleaming softly in the starlight, was the last remaining symbol of that struggle, and now, it too was ready to be put to rest.

Her companions stood with her, their faces solemn as they prepared to complete the final act of their long and arduous journey. They had fought together, had bled together, and had shared in the triumphs and tragedies that had brought them to this moment. And now, they were about to fulfill the prophecy that had guided them from the very beginning.

"Elara," Dain said softly, his voice breaking the silence. "Are you sure about this? We've been through so much to get the mirror. Are you ready to let it go?"

Elara turned to look at him, her heart swelling with gratitude for the man who had stood by her side through every trial. His concern was evident in his eyes, but so too was his trust in her, his belief that she would do what was right.

"I'm sure, Dain," Elara replied, her voice steady. "The mirror has served its purpose. It's time for it to rest, just as we must find peace after everything we've been through."

Lyra, ever the pragmatist, stepped forward, her sharp eyes fixed on the mirror. "You're right, Elara," she said. "The mirror is powerful, but it's also dangerous. We can't risk it falling into the wrong hands again."

Breck grunted in agreement, his expression grim. "Aye, we've seen what it can do—both the good and the bad. It's best if it stays hidden, where it can't be used for harm."

Tomas, the youngest of the group, looked uncertain, his gaze flicking between Elara and the mirror. "But... what if we need it again? What if something else happens, and we need its power to protect the kingdom?"

Elara smiled gently at him, understanding his fear. They had all come to rely on the mirror, to see it as the key to their victory, but she also knew that its power was not something that should be wielded lightly.

"The mirror is a tool of truth, Tomas," Elara said softly. "But the truth is something that lives within us, not in the mirror. We've all grown stronger, wiser, because of what we've been through. The mirror may have guided us, but it's up to us to carry that truth forward."

Tomas nodded slowly, his expression thoughtful as he considered her words. "I think I understand," he said finally. "We don't need the mirror anymore, because we've learned to trust ourselves."

Elara's heart swelled with pride as she looked at her companions, at the people who had become her family over the course of their journey. They had faced darkness, had confronted their deepest fears, and had emerged stronger for it. The prophecy had brought them together, had set them on this path, but now they were ready to forge their own destinies.

Taking a deep breath, Elara turned her gaze back to the mirror, its surface reflecting the light of the stars. The mirror's purpose had always been to reveal the truth, to guide those who sought to fulfill the prophecy. But now that the prophecy was fulfilled, its power was no longer needed. It was time to return the mirror to its resting place, to allow it to find peace just as they sought to do.

"Elara," Dain said softly, his voice filled with a mix of reverence and resolve. "It's time."

Elara nodded, her heart heavy with the weight of the moment. She had come so far, had grown so much, and now she was about to take the final step in fulfilling the prophecy that had shaped her life.

With a deep breath, Elara raised the Mirror of Eldoria, its surface glowing softly in the starlight. The clearing around them was bathed in the mirror's light, the trees casting long shadows that seemed to dance in the gentle breeze. The air was filled with a sense of anticipation, as if the very earth was holding its breath, waiting for what was to come.

"Elara of Briar Glen," a voice echoed softly in her mind, the voice of the Mirror's Keeper, though the Keeper was no longer present. "You have fulfilled your destiny, and in doing so, have brought balance to the kingdom. The mirror's purpose is complete, and now it must return to the earth from whence it came."

Elara closed her eyes, allowing the voice to guide her as she held the mirror aloft. She could feel the mirror's power pulsing beneath her fingers, a steady rhythm that matched the beating of her own heart. It was a reminder of everything they had been through, of the strength and courage they had found within themselves.

"The truth is within you, Elara," the voice continued, gentle and reassuring. "The mirror was only ever a reflection, a tool to help you see what was already there. Now, it is time for you to step into the light of your own truth, to embrace the destiny that is yours alone."

As the voice faded, Elara felt a surge of warmth spread through her, a sense of peace and acceptance that filled every corner of her being. She was no longer just a girl from a small village—she was a hero, a leader, someone who had faced the darkness and emerged into the light. She had fulfilled the prophecy, but more importantly, she had grown into her true self.

With a final, deep breath, Elara gently lowered the mirror, its light still glowing softly in the night. The clearing around them seemed to shimmer with a golden hue, the air filled with a sense of quiet reverence as if the very earth was acknowledging the significance of the moment.

"Elara," Dain said quietly, his voice filled with a mix of pride and emotion. "You've done it. You've fulfilled the prophecy."

Elara smiled, her heart swelling with love and gratitude for the man who had stood by her side through everything. "We've done it," she corrected softly. "We've all played a part in this, and we've all grown because of it."

Lyra stepped forward, her sharp eyes softened with emotion as she looked at Elara. "You're right, Elara. We've all changed, but it's because of you that we've made it this far. You led us, and you showed us the way."

Breck nodded, his expression grim but filled with a quiet pride. "Aye, you've been the heart of this group, Elara. We couldn't have done it without you."

Tomas, his eyes filled with admiration, added, "You're the reason we're all here, Elara. You've given us the strength to face our fears, to find our own truths."

Elara felt tears prick at the corners of her eyes as she looked at her companions, at the people who had become her family. She had led them on this journey, had guided them through the darkest of times, but she also knew that she wouldn't have made it without them. They had all played a part in fulfilling the prophecy, and they had all grown because of it.

With a final, deep breath, Elara turned her gaze back to the mirror, its light still glowing softly in her hands. The time had come to return the mirror to its resting place, to allow it to find peace just as they had.

Slowly, she lowered the mirror to the ground, the soft earth parting easily as she gently placed the mirror within it. The light from the mirror began to fade, its glow dimming as it settled into the earth, becoming one with the world once more.

The clearing around them seemed to sigh with relief, the tension that had filled the air slowly dissipating as the mirror's light faded completely. The stars above shone brightly, their light filling the clearing with a gentle, peaceful glow.

As Elara stepped back, she felt a deep sense of closure settle over her, a feeling of finality that brought with it a profound peace. The prophecy had been fulfilled, the mirror's purpose completed, and now it was time to move forward, to embrace the future that lay ahead.

"Elara," Dain said softly, his voice filled with emotion. "What happens now?"

Elara smiled, her heart light as she looked at the man who had become her closest friend, her protector, and perhaps something more. "Now, we live," she said simply. "We take what we've learned, the truths we've uncovered, and we use them to build a better future."

Lyra nodded, her expression filled with determination. "We've all changed, but that doesn't mean we can't continue to grow. We've faced the darkness, and now it's time to embrace the light."

Breck grunted in agreement, his expression resolute. "Aye, the kingdom still needs us. There's work to be done, and we'll face it together."

Tomas, his eyes bright with hope, added, "We've been through so much, but we're stronger for it. We can make a difference, we can help others find their own truths."

Elara's heart swelled with pride and love for her companions, for the people who had become her family. They had faced unimaginable challenges, had confronted their deepest fears, and had emerged stronger for it. Now, they were ready to move forward, to embrace the future with hope and determination.

As they left the clearing and made their way back to the kingdom, the night sky filled with the light of a thousand stars, Elara felt a deep sense of peace settle over her. The prophecy had been fulfilled, but more importantly, she had found her true self, had grown into the person she was always meant to be.

And as they walked together, side by side, Elara knew that whatever the future held, they would face it together. The mirror's power was no longer needed, its purpose fulfilled, but the truths they had uncovered would stay with them, guiding them as they built a new future, a future filled with hope, love, and the strength of their shared journey.

As they approached the kingdom's borders, the first light of dawn began to break over the horizon, casting the world in a warm, golden glow. The sun rose slowly, its light chasing away the shadows, bringing with it the promise of a new day, a new beginning.

And as Elara looked out at the world before her, at the kingdom she had fought to protect, she knew that they were ready to face whatever came next. They had fulfilled the prophecy, had embraced their destinies, and now, they were ready to build a future filled with hope, with love, and with the strength of their shared truth.

Together, they would face whatever challenges lay ahead, secure in the knowledge that they had the strength, the courage, and the love to overcome anything.

And as the sun rose higher in the sky, bathing the world in its warm, golden light, Elara knew that they had truly fulfilled the prophecy, in a way that no one had expected.

The End.

Did you love *The Enchanted Mirror*? Then you should read *The Phoenix King*[1] by Patrick William Lee!

The Phoenix King: unfolds the epic journey of a mythical ruler born from the Sacred Flame, destined to balance life and death. As he navigates trials of fire and confronts ancient evils, the Phoenix King must harness the Eternal Flame's power to restore harmony to his kingdom. From battling gods to merging with a dark counterpart, his quest reveals profound truths about sacrifice and renewal. This compelling saga weaves a tale of legacy, resilience, and the eternal cycle, inspiring generations to embrace balance and the unending dance of creation and destruction.

---

1. https://books2read.com/u/bQXlaZ

2. https://books2read.com/u/bQXlaZ

About the Author

Patrick William Lee is a renowned author celebrated for his enchanting tales of magic and wonder. Specializing in the genres of fairy tales, folk tales, legends, and mythology, Patrick weaves stories that transport readers to fantastical realms where the impossible becomes reality. With a deep love for folklore and a talent for crafting timeless narratives, his books captivate the imaginations of readers young and old. When he's not writing, Patrick enjoys exploring ancient forests, studying mythical creatures, and sharing his passion for storytelling with audiences around the world. His works continue to inspire and delight, leaving a lasting impact on the world of literature.